For Tim and Kristen and their families, all the people I love best

The

Mind

of a

Deviant

Woman

PAULA PAUL

outskirts
press

Outskirts Press, Inc.
http://www.outskirtspress.com

Paperback ISBN: 978-1-4787-9882-8
Hardback ISBN: 978-1-4787-9883-5

Cover Photo © 2018 gettyimages.com. All rights reserved - used with permission.

Outskirts Press and the "OP" logo are trademarks belonging to Outskirts Press, Inc.

PRINTED IN THE UNITED STATES OF AMERICA

To: William Van Patten, New York, New York
From: Louisa Van Patten, Charlottesville, Virginia
December 20, 1926

Dear Father,

I am in receipt of your letter, which you need not have written. You've made it quite clear several times in the past that you blame me for all that happened. I am surprised that your anger still burns after so much time has passed. You should have told me the truth long ago rather than keeping it hidden from me until it attacked me like a fierce beast when I unknowingly came upon its lair. If only you had told me, I could have followed a different path.

You say your motive in keeping the truth from me was to protect me. I wish with all of my heart that I could believe you, but I cannot see that you were protecting me. Rather, it seems you were protecting yourself and Mother and the Van Patten name and perhaps even Lemuel.

Now, it seems that none of us were protected. Not me nor you nor Mother and certainly not poor Lemuel. Could you not see that it would come to this? No, I think not. One cannot see when one's head is in the sand. Yet some good came of it as far as Lemuel and I are concerned, although you have made it clear that you do not agree.

I do not know how I shall ever make amends to Lemuel or how you will make amends to me or whether it is even necessary. However, I am doing all that I can to make some small if inadequate restitution to Carrie Buck. First, however, I must know the truth about her, and for that reason I have asked her to tell me her story. I can only hope that knowing will help me make restitution, and I can only pray that it is not too late.

In spite of all that has happened, I remain

Your daughter,
Louisa Van Patten

1

CARRIE

Sometimes I think I sort of remember being left with the Dobbs family back in 1909 when I was no more than three years old. But it could be I've been told about it so many times over the last five years that it only seemed like remembering.

Mr. Dobbs said he and Mrs. Dobbs took me in as an act of kindness. He was fond of reminding me of that. The reason for the act of kindness, Mrs. Dobbs said, was because my real mama wasn't fit to take care of me. "We adopted you out of the goodness of our hearts," Mrs. Dobbs said.

Goodness of our hearts. When I thought of a heart, I thought of a chicken's heart, bloody and no bigger than my thumb. Warm when I cleaved it out of a chicken that I killed for frying.

For a long time, I didn't remember one single thing about Mama, and I had no idea why she wasn't fit. Neither did I know that everything was about to change.

The last time things seemed normal was for a few hours one day when I was sitting in that bedroom I shared with Lucy. My scalp was purely aching as Mrs. Dobbs pulled at my hair. She was working it into a tight braid.

Lucy sat on the bed staring at her own face in a hand mirror,

---

pinching her cheeks and biting her lips to make them turn red and ignoring me when I cried out in pain.

Lucy was the Dobbses' real daughter. She was nine years older than me. I can still remember when I first came; the two of us would play games and play with Lucy's dolls.

By the time Lucy was nineteen, she hardly noticed me at all. At least Waverly still noticed me. He was Lucy's seventeen-year-old brother, the only person I ever really liked. Maybe that was because he was the only person who seemed to like me.

"Hold still, child," Mrs. Dobbs said that day. She gave my hair another yank. "I swear you got hair as fine as cat hair. Can't hardly control it. But I ain't takin' you out unless you look halfway decent."

I surely didn't want to risk Mrs. Dobbs leaving me at home when she went shopping down on Main Street. I wasn't about to miss out on getting the new dress that she promised me to start a new school year. It would be the only dress I'd ever had that Lucy hadn't worn first. Mrs. Dobbs said I deserved a new dress this year since I was doing so well in school. Oh yes, she could be kind sometimes, and it wasn't that I disliked her. I was pretty sure Mrs. Dobbs didn't dislike me either. It was mostly that there just was no kind of warmth between us.

Lucy would probably get a new dress, too. Not for school, of course. Lucy had quit school after her first year of high school. Now that she was nineteen and had no prospects for marriage, the Dobbses worried that she would be an old maid. I overheard them more than once talking about it in the kitchen after they thought everyone else was asleep.

Well, when my hair was finally braided and pulled so tight it made my eyes look slanted, the three of us made the short walk from the Dobbses' house on Grove Street, across the railroad tracks to Main Street. We had just come out of the J. C. Penney store, where all the dresses we'd looked at cost too much, when Mrs. Dobbs grabbed my hand.

That sure surprised me. She usually only took my hand if we were crossing the street. She always said it was dangerous enough that everybody had to dodge all those horses and buggies, but nowadays it was motor cars that worried her. Mr. Dobbs would try to calm her fear by reminding her that Charlottesville didn't have more than a handful of those automobiles on the streets in the first place, and they didn't move much faster than the buggies in the second place, although he did admit that they made loud noises. Mrs. Dobbs said they sounded like somebody farting.

Mrs. Dobbs jerked my arm and pulled me back into the store. Before she did that, though, she hesitated just long enough for me to look up at her face and see that she was frowning at something ahead of her. I followed her gaze and saw a woman several yards away staring back at us. The woman had dark hair like mine, but it wasn't braided as mine was. It wasn't put up in a pompadour like Mrs. Dobbs's either. It was messy. The woman was kind of round and plump like Mrs. Dobbs. Her face was round, too, and she looked like she was mad at somebody. Later I thought maybe she just looked sad. Her dress wasn't any color at all, and it was too short. It didn't even cover her ankles.

I wanted to ask who that woman was, why she was looking at us that way, and why Mrs. Dobbs pulled me back into the store. I didn't ask, though, because I knew questions like that made Mrs. Dobbs angry. Children should be seen, not heard, she said.

"That woman we saw was your real mother," Lucy told me later. She whispered it because she didn't want Mrs. Dobbs to hear. I was so surprised I didn't know what to say. I knew I had a mother somewhere, a woman who had caused the Dobbses to have to resort to "an act of kindness." I always pictured her frail and sick—someone who couldn't take care of her daughter—and very beautiful, of course. Golden-haired and sweet-faced like Mary Pickford. I never had seen a moving picture at that time, but I knew who Mary Pickford was. Lucy pointed out her picture on a big sign just outside the Paramount Theater.

"Why are you looking at me like that?" Lucy asked.

"My mother?" That was all I could say.

"Shhh," Lucy said, looking over her shoulder toward the bedroom door. "Don't let on you know who she is."

3

I didn't get the chance to ask Lucy why I wasn't supposed to know because I had to help get supper on the table, and I just never got up the courage to talk to Lucy about her after that. I did ask Waverly once. He said he didn't know anything about my mama, so I never asked him again. When I think back on it, I believe he was lying because he didn't want me to know my mama was a prostitute.

I saw Mama again a few months later. This time she had two kids with her. Both of them looked younger than me. And this time Mrs. Dobbs didn't have time to pull me into a store.

"Afternoon, Miz Dobbs," my mama said.

All Mrs. Dobbs said was "Miz Buck," and it came out like she was trying to keep from choking.

"This Carrie?" the woman asked. She was looking right at me. I felt like something was leapfrogging over my heart.

Mrs. Dobbs told her yes, turning the word into a hiss.

"She grew some."

She smiled when she said that. Then it seemed as if nobody could think of anything else to say. All I did was stare at those two kids—a boy and a girl. The boy appeared to be maybe three or four years old, and he was as dark-haired and dark-eyed as his mama. His runny nose had made a white crust around his nostrils. The britches he wore were as dirty as any I ever saw, and the knees needed patching. The girl was older, maybe six. She had dark hair, too, but her eyes were gray. Her face was all streaked, making me think she'd been crying. I kept trying to get the girl to look at me, but she would only look at the sidewalk. She was wearing dirty britches, too, just like her brother. That made me feel embarrassed because Mrs. Dobbs said it wasn't proper for a girl or woman to wear britches, much less dirty ones.

After a while, it seemed Mrs. Dobbs couldn't tolerate everybody just standing there not saying anything because she said something like "I trust you're doing well."

"Wouldn't say that," Mama said. "Been laid up in the county hospital with pneumonia. State put the kids in the orphans' home till I got out." She looked at me again and said, "This here's your brother Roy and your sister Doris."

I could see Mrs. Dobbs out of the corner of my eye, saw her lips get thin and white.

All of a sudden I asked my mama if she was feeling all right by now. I was as surprised as anybody to hear the words coming out of my mouth, but I was truly worried about my mama being in the hospital.

"Gettin' by," Mama said.

"Well, if there's anything you need..."

I felt a jerk on my arm and heard Mrs. Dobbs say, "If you'll excuse us, Mrs. Buck, we've got to be going. The girl has chores to finish, and there's school tomorrow."

I did my best to hang back and look over my shoulder at my mama, but she had already turned away with the two kids following her.

"You are not to speak unless you are spoken to," Mrs. Dobbs said that night, "especially not to that loose woman."

Loose woman. I kept thinking of a woman who was supposed to be chained to a stake the way some people did their dogs, or kept in a pen behind the house like horses and milk cows. People said they were loose when they got out of their chains or over fences.

I saw Mama a few times after that, but it was never for very long, and there was never time to say much. I don't think I hardly spoke at all to the boy and girl who were supposed to be my brother and sister. Roy was quiet and stuck close to his mama. Doris still didn't seem to want to look at me. She couldn't stand still, and several times she wandered off so Mama had to go find her. Mama never looked healthy, although she was always plump. She had a pale face, and more than once I saw her limping or rubbing an arm and complaining about rheumatism. I wanted more than anything to help her, maybe buy her some medicine at the drugstore, but I had no money of my own. The best I could do was go to sleep at night dreaming of how someday I'd be rich enough to buy Mama and Doris and Roy a house and food and medicine.

If the way to get rich is to work hard, like some people say, I thought I was in luck because I already knew how to work hard. I worked every day in the kitchen, in the garden, and at the laundry tubs. Sometimes I was too tired to do my homework for school. I knew I didn't have any right to complain though. As Mr. and Mrs. Dobbs said, I had to earn my keep.

"Be grateful you have a roof over your head, clothes on your back, and plenty to eat," Mrs. Dobbs was fond of saying.

I suppose I was content back then. Mrs. Dobbs rarely scolded me, and she didn't whip me any more often than other people whipped their own kids. One thing I did wish I could have, though, was a doll like Lucy had when she was my age. I never did mention it to the Dobbses. I didn't want them to think I was ungrateful for their act of kindness.

Besides, I understood that I wasn't really a member of the family and that Mr. and Mrs. Dobbs didn't have the same love for me as they did for Lucy and Waverly. But the Dobbses were mostly kind to me, and I didn't know what more I could ask for.

One good thing was that I had friends at school who seemed to like me at least as much as the Dobbses did, even though they'd never had to perform any acts of kindness for me.

One of my friends was Davy Hopkins. He was in my grade at the McGuffy School. He took to walking home with me after school since he lived only a block from the Dobbses' little frame house on Grove Street. That was fine with me. I liked having someone to talk to on the way home. I wouldn't have minded walking home with Waverly, but he quit school just after Lucy quit. Now he was working at the lumberyard.

School had been in session less than two months when Davy announced that he was going to skip school the next day. I didn't say anything back to him, and after a while he said, "You wanna know why?"

At the time I was looking at the little shoots of grass that had bullied their way up from the cracks in the sidewalk because it had been such a warm fall, so all I did was shrug.

"I'm going fishin' over at the river. They's a good spot I know over there." After another long wait, he said. "You wanna go?"

I told him I didn't know if I wanted to or not. The truth was I wasn't too interested right then because I'd spied a pink lady slipper that was still blooming. It was dark pink and fleshy like a person's tongue.

Davy wasn't about to give up. "What you mean you don't know?"

"Never been fishin'," I told him.

"Well, it's fun. I could show you how."

That got my attention. I truly liked learning new stuff, and I'd heard fishing was purely enjoyable. "Would you?" I asked.

"Sure," he said.

Pretty soon I was having second thoughts, and I reminded him that if we went fishing, we'd have to miss school.

The humph sound Davy made reminded me of an old man. "You mean you never played hooky?" he asked

I wasn't going to admit I'd never played hooky, but I'd heard other kids talking about it. It was mostly the boys who did it. I remember one of them talking about how he'd sneaked off into the woods with a kid in a grade higher than he was, and how they'd had a picnic of cold biscuits and jam made from wild strawberries.

"You scared a worms?" Davy asked.

I told him I wasn't, but the truth was I didn't know whether I was or not. I never had much to do with worms, unless you count weevils that got in flour sometimes.

"Then let's go!" he said.

It wasn't easy getting four of the cold leftover biscuits out of the house, and I had to settle for apple butter to spread between them since there was no wild strawberry jam to be had. Davy was waiting for me the next morning behind the grocery store, just where he said he'd be. He'd brought two poles and a can of worms, and I had the biscuits wrapped in a tea towel.

Davy was right. It was fun. Part of the time we played tag and splashed each other with river water. When we got down to serious fishing, Davy showed me how to get a worm on a hook for bait and how and where to drop my line in the water. I caught on fast, and it wasn't too long before I got a feeling of knowing just where the fish would be. I caught four fish to Davy's two, but I had to give them to Davy. There would be no possible way to explain to Mr. and Mrs. Dobbs how I got the four fish without lying. Mrs. Dobbs always said lying was an abomination. I didn't know that word, *abomination*. Lucy said it meant someone was going to hell. Davy said it was another word for a cow's stomach. Anyway, I didn't keep the fish.

I found out that I liked fishing, though, and me and Davy skipped school a few more times that year after the weather got warm again. Once, two other girls and another boy met us down at the river. No one fished that time. We played Kick the Can and Red Rover until everyone was almost too tired to walk home.

Playing hooky ended when I got caught passing a note to Davy.

Big fireballs shaped like words came out of Miss Watson's mouth in a loud blast that I could have sworn burned her face when she shouted, "What are you doing, Carrie?"

I mumbled that I wasn't doing nothing and crumpled the note in my fist. I was afraid to look up at Miss Watson's narrow face and skinny frame, but she pried the note out of my hand and walked to the front of the classroom. I glanced up long enough to see the big, fat coiled snake that was Miss Watson's knotted hair at the back of her head. I knew what was coming next and slumped down in my seat, wishing I could disappear while the teacher read the note aloud.

Dear Davy,

Meet me tomorrow in the woods next to the river so no one can see us.

Carrie Buck
P.S. Don't let anybody else come.

The room seemed like it was flickering with all the snickering that was going on. Miss Watson put a stop to it by giving everyone ten extra arithmetic problems for homework. It was the worst thing that could have happened.

"Why'd you have to get us all in trouble, Horseface?"

"We didn't do nothin', and because of you we get extra homework."

"Yeah, Horseface, I hate you."

"Was you and Davy going to sneak in the woods and kiss?"

"Not kiss, you dummy. They was going to fuck."

"Fuck? What's that mean?"

I ran home as fast as I could. I hated them flinging all that anger at me. I hated anything that made me the center of attention. Most of all, though, I hated being called Horseface. Raymond Hamilton was the one who started it. He said it was because my face was long and narrow like a horse's, and my hair was black and straight like a horse's mane.

I dreaded going home because I was certain Mrs. Dobbs would have learned what happened somehow, but when I got there, no one said anything about it. I was in the kitchen, washing the supper dishes and thinking the story of my dreadful sin hadn't spread beyond the third grade, when someone knocked on the door. Mr. Dobbs put down his paper to see who was there and opened the door to Miss Watson. I recognized her voice but kept my back turned to the door leading from the kitchen to the living room. I kept my hands in the dishpan, wishing I could get my entire body in that murky water.

I heard the awful truth coming in little bursts: "I'm sorry to have to bring this...ahem, excuse me but...She was passing it to a boy, you say? Oh my! You don't suppose...? Of course she'll be disciplined. You understand that this need not go any further. You should not have to suffer the embarrassment, Mr. and Mrs. Dobbs, because after all it was an act of kindness on your part to—"

"Carrie! Come here, please," bellowed Mr. Dobbs from the living room.

I went to the living room, head down, with my hands still stinging from the dishwashing soap Mrs. Dobbs made with lye.

"Do you recognize this?" He showed me the note I'd written.

"Yes sir."

"What is the meaning...?

"I don't know."

"Give me a proper answer."

I was too scared to speak at first. All I could do was look down at my chapped and stinging hands folded in front of me. "I was gonna play hooky," I said finally.

"Hooky, you say? You were going to play hooky? Look at me when you speak."

I raised my head but only high enough to see Mr. Dobbs's big stomach with a white shirt and black vest stretched across it. The vest buttons were struggling to hold on.

"How many times have you skipped school, and what were you doing when you should have been in school?"

I had to swallow hard before I could mumble an answer.

"Fishing? You've skipped school to go fishing? How many times?"

In the end I had to stay home from school for the rest of the week. I did the laundry, scrubbing everything on the washboard until my knuckles were bleeding. I did all of the ironing, a month's worth, sweating until my hair was stiff because I had to stay in the hot kitchen and heat the flatirons on the stove. I washed all of the windows and fell off the ladder once. My elbow hurt so bad I thought for two days that it was broken.

I would have rather taken a whipping.

2

CARRIE

Waverly laughed when he heard about the trouble I got into because of the note. "You gotta learn to be careful, kid. Don't let nobody see you passing notes. What you do is, you put it under your shoe but don't let nobody see you do that, then slide it to whoever you're sending it to. Like this, see?" He moved his foot real slow. "Now I mean it when I say don't let nobody see you, and I ain't talkin' about just the teacher. There'll be snitches watchin', and you got to know who they are. You get to where you can pick 'em out even before they snitch. You can just tell. Like Lucy. She was one of them snitches when she was in school."

"I appreciate your advice," I said, "but I probably won't ever do it again. Pass notes, I mean."

He laughed again. "Not until you get to want to go fishin', that is. I can tell how much you like to fish."

"Well..."

"Don't worry about it, kid," he said and ruffled my hair. "Anybody as good a fisherman as you can't be all bad."

"How'd you know I was good at it?"

Waverly laughed. "Davy Hopkins said it." He laughed again. "He was pure jealous 'cause you caught more than him."

"Well, thanks for the compliment," I called to his back as he walked away. He was on his way to work, although he kept saying he was going to quit the lumberyard job and find something better. Another reason I liked Waverly was that he was the only one who didn't have a million chores for me, the way Mr. and Mrs. Dobbs did, and he wasn't always complaining about my manners as Lucy did.

It wasn't always bad. I hope you understand that. There were some good days like the Christmas a couple of years later when I got Annabelle.

Annabelle had pinkish skin on her porcelain arms and face and a soft body filled up with cotton. Her hair was black, and the way it was painted on her head reminded me of a little cap. She wore a blue-checkered gingham dress and had black shoes painted on her little feet at the end of her floppy legs. When I unwrapped my package on Christmas morning and saw her for the first time, it made me think that maybe Santa Claus, or God, (back then I more or less thought they were one and the same) had forgiven me for writing a note to Davy and for playing hooky. It was the only time I ever got anything for Christmas, except socks and underwear and once a pair of patent leather shoes.

That year, Lucy got a jacket trimmed with fur that almost looked real. Of course she was too big for dolls, but she had plenty of them all lined up on a shelf on her side of the room; some had painted faces and some had their features stitched on. Annabelle was the only doll I ever had, and I wasn't about to put her up on that shelf to collect dust. Her place when she wasn't with me was leaning against the pillow on my side of the bed.

"It looks like you just dropped that thing there and forgot about it. Makes the whole room look messy," Lucy said.

The first time I entered the room and saw that Annabelle wasn't propped against my pillow, I screamed because I thought she was gone.

Hearing the scream, Mrs. Dobbs hurried down the hall, crying, "Lord 'a' mercy." I never had seen her come that close to running. She looked kind of funny with her wide hips quaking and her hair slithering out of its pompadour. "What's wrong with you, girl?" she asked. She had a hand on her chest and was gasping like she was having a heart attack.

I was sobbing so much I had a hard time telling her Annabelle was gone

"Annabelle? Who's Annabelle?" she asked.

Lucy came up behind her mother and said, "She's talking about her dumb old doll, Mama." Mrs. Dobbs still looked as if she didn't understand, so Lucy said, "I put it up there—on the shelf."

I looked to where she was pointing, and there was Annabelle on the end of the shelf, leaning toward the edge like she was about to fall off. I hadn't thought to look up there, and seeing her that way made me cry even harder. Mrs. Dobbs grabbed me by the shoulders. "Get ahold of yourself, Carrie," she said. "That's no cause for you to have a fit."

I managed to jerk myself loose and climbed up on the bed so I could reach the shelf and rescue Annabelle. Mrs. Dobbs about had a stroke. "Get off the bed, Carrie," she said. "You know I don't allow that! Now straighten that bedspread."

All I could do was stand there on the bed and hug Annabelle, burying my face in her soft, boneless body. Mrs. Dobbs yelled again, telling me to hush that bawling and straighten up the bed, but she also told Lucy to leave my doll alone from then on. Lucy got a little whiny and told her mama she was just trying to keep the room looking nice.

"I know, honey, but you know how she is about that doll," Mrs. Dobbs said. Then she told me again to hush up and go to the kitchen and peel the potatoes for supper.

After that I made a little bed for Annabelle out of an apple crate. I shoved the crate under the bed so Lucy couldn't say it made the room look messy. Every night I took Annabelle out of her crate and slept with her clutched up close. I took Annabelle with me almost everywhere I went. I would have even taken her to school if it hadn't been against the rules.

Once I had her cradled in her arm as me and the Dobbses walked home from church. All of them, that is, except Waverly. He'd quit going by then.

The words to the last hymn they'd sung were stuck in my head.

What can wash away my sin?
Nothing but the blood of Jesus.
Oh precious is the flow
That makes me white as snow.
Nothing but the blood of Jesus.

I hated having that song stuck in my mind because I thought it would be sickening to be washed in anybody's blood. That was what I was thinking when I saw Mama. She was walking toward all of us with Doris and Roy following her. This time she wore a dress that looked almost new. It was blue and flecked with little yellow flowers, but it didn't fit her very well. It was baggy, even on her stout body. Doris had a dress, too, but she was so skinny that anything would look baggy on her. Roy looked to be wearing the trousers with the worn knees that Doris must have outgrown. They were all walking past the grocery store, which was closed on Sundays. Roy and Doris stopped and pressed their noses to the front glass and stared inside.

Mr. and Mrs. Dobbs saw them right about then. Mrs. Dobbs mumbled something I couldn't understand, and she started to turn around and head back toward the church. She was stopped in her tracks when Mr. Dobbs touched the brim of his hat and said, "How do, Emma."

Mrs. Dobbs said real low, "I swanie, J. T." But she put on a kind of fake smile and nodded to all three of them. I wanted more than anything to say hello to my mama, but I felt too timid.

Mama spoke to the Dobbses. "The girl looks fit enough," she said, looking at me.

The girl. Couldn't she have used my name? After all, she was the one who chose it. Or was she? Maybe it was my daddy who chose it. The one Mr. Dobbs said died in some kind of accident. Mama kept talking, and I wanted to hear more of whatever she said, but I could feel Doris looking at me.

She pointed to Annabelle and said, "Where'd you get that?"

"Santa brought it."

Doris curled her lip the way people do when something stinks. "They ain't no Santa. That woman must have give it to you."

"You mean Mrs. Dobbs?"

"Mrs. Dobbs? How come you don't call her Mama?"

"'Cause she ain't my real mama."

Doris curled her lip again. "She 'dopted you, didn't she? That makes her your mama."

"Well, she said it wouldn't be right for me to call her Mama. She said I should call her Mrs. Dobbs, and I should say Mr. Dobbs, not Papa." I guess I sounded smart-alecky, but Doris was the one who started it.

She couldn't seem to keep her eyes off of Annabelle. "Call her whatever, but she's the one give you the doll 'cause they ain't no such a thing as Santa."

"Then I don't know where she came from," I said. Doris's words hadn't shocked me. Not really. I'd recently started to suspect that Santa wasn't real. I wasn't sure about God yet.

"I seen prettier ones," Doris said. She reached out her hand and touched Annabelle's painted hair. Her hand was real little, and it was streaked with dirt. I pulled Annabelle away from her.

"Her name's Annabelle." I was purposely talking like a smart-aleck by this time.

Mama was walking away by then, and Doris and Roy had to follow her. Doris looked back over her shoulder and said, "Stupid name."

"Is not! You're the one that's stupid," I said.

Mrs. Dobbs pulled my arm and told me to behave. In spite of the angry sound of her voice when she spoke to me, I saw soon enough that it was Mr. Dobbs she was mad at.

"Now see what you started, J. T.," she said. "I don't see why you have to speak to every criminal you see. Just because you're a constable. Especially her. Why do you think you have to speak to her?"

Mr. Dobbs said he figured Emma was no worse than the rest of them, and Mrs. Dobbs made a snorting sound.

She leaned close to Mr. Dobbs and told him in a voice she thought I couldn't hear that he knew very good and well what that woman was. It made me wonder. Whatever Mama was, it was something Mrs. Dobbs didn't approve of. I knew my mama wasn't a Negro, so she had to be either a Jew or a Republican.

3

CARRIE

When Lucy came home late on a Saturday night in early March of 1916 and told us she was getting married, Mr. Dobbs sat up straighter in his chair and let his newspaper drop to the floor.

Mrs. Dobbs's response was "Well, my Lord! Who?"

"Tom, who else would you think it would be?" Lucy sounded like she couldn't believe her mother said that. I could understand why she felt that way. After all, Tom Pote was the only man who had courted her recently. He would come by in his sputtering motor car, which he referred to as his tin lizzie, and take Lucy away. Then he'd bring her back in a few hours all dusty and windblown.

Mr. Dobbs rose from his chair. "Tom Pote from over at Manassas? Works at the rail yard over there?" He spoke the words as if it was the most amazing thing he could imagine.

"Oh yes!" Mrs. Dobbs took a step toward Lucy. "Tom. He's such a nice boy."

"Man, Mama, he ain't a boy. He's twenty-five." Lucy was smiling as she spoke. Mrs. Dobbs put her arms around her and hugged her close.

"I'm just so happy for you," Mrs. Dobbs said.

Mr. Dobbs mumbled something that sounded like "Thank the Lord."

If I hadn't been afraid of getting swatted, I might have said the same thing. No one could be any happier at the thought of having Lucy out of the house than I was. It meant I could have the bedroom all to myself, and I wouldn't have to keep Annabelle under the bed anymore.

I still kept her pulled close to my chest every night, and I whispered things to her when I knew Lucy was asleep. I told her the same thing every night. "You're my little girl, and I'm your mama, and I'll never ever give you away."

For the first two weeks after Lucy told everyone she was getting married, I had several nights to talk to Annabelle since Lucy was either out with Tom or at one of her friend's homes talking about her wedding plans.

The wedding was to be at the Dobbses' house. Lucy's two closest friends would be there, and Mr. Dobbs's sister and her family would come, as well as other family members and neighbors. Counting the preacher and his wife, there would be twenty people for supper after the ceremony.

Because the house had to be cleaned from top to bottom, and because a number of pies and cakes had to be baked ahead of time, I hardly had time to keep up with my schoolwork during the last two weeks of March.

On Friday, the day of the wedding, I spent the morning helping Mrs. Dobbs cut up chickens to fry later in the day. The various chicken parts rested in pans of cool water set atop a block of ice Mr. Dobbs had brought home from the icehouse on the edge of town. Lucy was supposed to help out in the kitchen, too, but she didn't do much except stare out the window at the willow tree and poke her finger into the filling of one of the cherry pies I had baked the night before. I went to the trouble of making a lattice crust, making sure each strip was exactly the same size. Now Lucy had broken one of the strips near the edge.

She had a dress of light-blue georgette taffeta with a tiered skirt that only came down to her ankles and new patent leather shoes with pointed toes. She ordered both the dress and the shoes from the Montgomery Ward catalog. What she really wanted was a dark-blue dress with sheer silk sleeves, but it was too expensive, and Mrs. Dobbs said she shouldn't wear such a dark color for a wedding anyway.

By eleven o'clock Lucy had disappeared from the kitchen, saying she had to start getting dressed, even though the wedding wasn't until three o'clock. Time must have been flowing uphill for her, judging by the way she kept coming downstairs to check the clock in the living room. For me, though, time was passing so fast, like it was rolling down a steep cliff. I barely had time to get to the bedroom to change into my best dress, a yellow serge pinafore, even if it had once belonged to Lucy. I'd outgrown my new dress a long time ago.

"Oh, Carrie, that dress is too small for you! Don't you have anything else to wear?" Lucy sounded as if she was about to cry. That surprised me. Lucy usually paid no attention to what I wore.

"It's my only good dress." I was struggling to button the waist. "I guess I grew some." I might have saved my breath since Lucy was no longer listening. She was concentrating on painting something black on her eyebrows, while her friend Julia kept wiping off the paint with a handkerchief and instructing her to start over again and not paint with such wide strokes. Another friend, Audrey, was trying to make dainty crimped waves along the sides of Lucy's dark hair.

"Carrie, fetch me a glass of water," Audrey said. "I'm going to have to dampen the sides again to make the waves set."

"Just a minute," I said, trying to pull on my shoes and stockings. I was sitting on the floor since Lucy was seated on the only chair in front of the dresser, and the bed was stacked with the clothes she'd pulled out to transfer to the house where she and Tom would live.

"Carrie! Hurry!" Lucy's voice was screechy. "You can do that later. It's almost time to start!"

"I have to put my shoes on. I can't go to a wedding without my shoes, and I haven't even combed my—"

"I said hurry!" Lucy was making another attempt to paint her eyebrow, and there was sweat on her forehead.

"Oh all right!" I snapped at her and grabbed a comb from the dresser. I hobbled out of the room, carrying one shoe and stocking in one hand and trying to comb my hair with the other as I rushed to the kitchen.

"Hey! How come you're just wearing one shoe?"

I glanced in the direction of the voice and saw that it had come from Clarence, Mr. Dobbs's nephew. He was a little older than me, already twelve, and I hated him.

"None of your business!" I didn't look at him as I took a glass from the cupboard and started working the handle on the pump.

"Your buttons are gaping in the front. You look stupid. You ought to get a bigger dress."

"Shut up!" I said, still not looking at him as I hurried out of the kitchen. I could hear Clarence snickering behind me.

By the time I got the glass of water to Audrey and finished dressing, Mrs. Dobbs was calling for me to help with the last-minute details in the kitchen. I was still setting out glasses—most of them borrowed from neighbors—when I heard the preacher clear his throat and announce that the guests should be seated and that the bride and groom should step forward.

The preacher looked different from when he stood behind the pulpit or lingered at the front door of the church to shake hands with people as they left. Somehow the small living room with its dark damask curtains and filled with chairs from the kitchen made Pastor Ingersal look too big for the room. He wasn't just "stout" as Mrs. Dobbs had once described him; he was as overstuffed as the fading sofa where Mr. and Mrs. Dobbs now sat. Mr. Dobbs was in the dark-blue suit he always wore to church. It had been pressed so many times with a hot iron and damp cloth that it now had a shine to it that reminded me of fish scales. Mrs. Dobbs had on her good dress, the one with little sprigs of green ivy on a white background.

By the time I stepped into the living room, there were no chairs left unoccupied, and some of the people were standing. Waverly and Clarence, as well as Audrey, were standing along the wall directly across from me. Waverly wore a new pair of trousers he'd bought with the money he'd made working at his new job in the Western Union office. He also had on a white shirt and a tie. He had dampened his hair so the sandy color had turned brown, and he'd parted it and combed it to the side, making a deep wave at the front. I had never seen him looking so handsome, and I couldn't pull my eyes away from him until the preacher spoke.

"Let us begin with prayer," the preacher said. I bowed my head along with everyone else in the room. The preacher asked God to bless Lucy and Tom and to bless them with children and to make them raise the kids right. He asked for protection from harm and droned on about salvation and about heaven and hell. Keeping my head down for so long made me feel sleepy, so I opened my eyes and lifted my head to look at Waverly again. He still had his head bowed, but he was grinning and whispering something to Audrey. Whatever he'd said made Audrey put a hand over her mouth to keep from giggling. Waverly put his hand on her waist, and I felt a wave of jealousy wash over me. I wanted Waverly to whisper things to me, not Audrey—things that would make me giggle and make him touch me.

It was only then that I noticed Clarence was looking at me. He had a disgusting grin on his face. Still looking at me, he pursed his lips and then licked them. I ducked my head and closed my eyes and never looked up again until the long prayer was over. Finally, when the prayer ended and I glanced at Lucy, she looked almost beautiful in her new dress and her nicely styled hair. Tom looked stiff and frightened and could barely say "I do" when the time came.

The ceremony was short, not nearly as long as the prayer, and all too soon I had to leave the room to heat the grease and fry the chickens that were still cooling in the pans of water. Mrs. Dobbs's sister, Clarence's mother, came in to help, along with two of the neighbor women. Their presence gave me no comfort. I wanted to be in the living room with Waverly.

I could hear bits of conversation while I worked in the kitchen. Most of it seemed to be about a war that was going on somewhere on the other side of the ocean. Some of the men said the United States ought to help out. Others said it wasn't our war, and we ought not to stick our noses in other people's business. Waverly wouldn't be talking about a war; I was sure. He'd be telling a funny story about something that happened at the Western Union office or something just as funny that someone said when he delivered a telegram.

There would be no going to the living room for me until all of the chicken was cooked, though, and there would be nothing to break the monotony in the kitchen unless you count Clarence coming in and swatting my behind with a rolled-up dish towel. I let out a yelp and wished I could splash hot grease on him, but I didn't do anything. Clarence's mother didn't do anything either, except laugh and shoo Clarence out, saying boys will be boys, which was just about the dumbest thing I could imagine anybody saying.

When at last the meal was cooked and spread on the table waiting for guests to fill their plates, I ventured into the living room. I felt sticky from sweat, and I knew damp strands of hair stuck to my face. No one noticed, though, certainly not Waverly, who had left Audrey's side and was talking to his uncle and two of the neighbor men.

"Hell yes, I'll go," he said. A piece of his hair had separated from the wave in front and hung down the middle of his forehead, giving him a kind of careless look. His eyes looked a little blurry, too. I'd seen him that way once before when he'd come home very late from his job. I'd met him at the back door on my way out to the privy. He'd whispered to me that he had drunk a little whiskey and that I was not to tell anyone. I never told, and I loved the idea that the two of us had a secret.

Did those blurry eyes mean he'd been drinking whiskey again? If so, where did he get it? The Dobbses had made it clear that there would be no alcohol at the wedding.

I moved a little closer to Waverly and the group of men.

"You don't know what you're talking about, Waverly," one of

them said. "You don't want to go over there and fight no war. Have them Germans shooting bullets at you? No siree."

"I sure as hell do," Waverly said. "I'm fixin' to join the army."

All of a sudden I felt empty. Like my heart had leaped from my body. Until that moment I'd never heard anything worse.

4

CARRIE

"I was going to be drafted anyway, so just leave me alone," Waverly said when Mrs. Dobbs found out he had joined the army. That was in March 1917. I remember because Lucy had been married almost a year and had already lost her first baby, who was only a few weeks old. By that time I'd started to think Waverly had forgotten about joining the army.

"What do you know about war?" she asked.

Waverly shrugged. "I can shoot a gun,"

"Well, that don't make no difference. You sure don't know how to kill people." There was a screechy quiver in her voice.

"Reckon I can learn."

"Oh my Lord, boy! What are you saying?" By now Mrs. Dobbs was having a full-fledged fit. Her face was red, and it looked like she was going to hit Waverly with the big spoon she had in her hand.

"I ain't no boy, Mama."

"You ain't but twenty."

"I'll be twenty-one next month, and anyway, somebody's got to go whup them Germans."

"You could of waited though. You didn't have to go—"

"I didn't wait, Mama. It's done and over with."

Waverly stalked out, slamming the back door behind him, leaving Mrs. Dobbs crying and carrying on like she'd just had her arm chopped off. There wasn't a thing I could do to comfort her because I was about to cry. I bit my lip hard enough to make it bleed.

He left within a few weeks to learn how to fight a war. The day he left, he hugged his mama and shook hands with his daddy. I stood back, watching. When he looked at me and walked toward me, I thought for sure he was going to kiss me, or at least hug me. All he did was ruffle my hair and say, "Take care of yourself, kid."

He was supposed to come home one more time after that, but it turned out he didn't get to. The way I understood it, President Wilson got in a big hurry to send soldiers to France, and that's where Waverly went. I'd heard of France from geography class at school, but I didn't really know much about it except that it was far away and there was a war there.

Whenever people stopped by the house or Mrs. Dobbs saw someone she knew in town, they would always say things like "Don't worry; he'll be all right" or "The war will be over soon" or "I'm praying for your boy." It seemed to me that Mrs. Dobbs would just as soon not hear anybody say anything. I know I felt that way. The only way I could stand it was just to not think about it.

That's also the way I got by when it came to Mama and Doris and Roy. I tried not to think about them too much so I wouldn't start feeling sorry for them and for me. Then when I happened to see them, which wasn't very often, I felt sad and happy at the same time.

When school closed in June that year, my fifth grade year, I was getting along okay. Not happy, maybe, but not too bad either. The day school was out and I got my final report card was the day I guess I came the closest to being happy. I couldn't wait to show the card to Mr. and Mrs. Dobbs.

I had passed all of my subjects, but I was particularly proud of the note Miss Nelson wrote at the bottom of the card. I liked her much better than I did old Miss Watson in the fourth grade.

Very good in deportment and lessons, the note said. I thought both Mr. and Mrs. Dobbs would be proud of me. I was pretty sure that even though Lucy had always passed all of her subjects, she never got such a note.

Mrs. Dobbs's response wasn't quite what I expected though. She took the card I handed her, gave it a glance and a nod of her head, tossed it on the kitchen table, and told me to snap the beans and put them on to cook with a little salt pork.

I did as I was told, but I left the card on the table for Mr. Dobbs to see when he came home. It did no good. He didn't notice it, and Mrs. Dobbs didn't mention it. Neither did I because I was afraid it would make me seem boastful. Still, I was proud of that report card. That night I put it in one of Mr. Dobbs's old discarded cigar boxes where I kept my favorite things like the ribbon that had tied the package Annabelle came in, a dried flower I thought was extra pretty, and a picture of Mary Pickford I tore out of a *Life Magazine*.

I remember how hard I worked that summer after the fifth grade. There was so much cooking, cleaning, laundry, mending, gardening, and canning vegetables for the winter that I didn't have time to think, except I kept wishing Lucy was there to help out. Not that she'd ever been much help, and by now, of course, she'd moved away with Tom. I didn't mind her being gone so much. It meant that if I ever did get a few minutes of my own, I could go to our bedroom and she wouldn't be there. I could pull out my cigar box and take a peek at the report card. *Recommended for promotion to sixth grade*, it said. It made me want the summer to end and school to start so I could progress even more in my education.

August that year was extra hot and sticky. There were times when I thought I'd pass out in that steamy kitchen full of Mason jars sitting in pressurized steam. Not a single breath of air would favor me by blowing through the one small open window. I wasn't allowed to open the door because there was no screen on it, and flies could come in. I don't think even a fly would want to buzz into that hot kitchen though. Not when it could fly around outdoors where there was at least a breeze sometimes.

Mrs. Dobbs helped with the canning. It was so hot her pompadour loosened and fell down in wet strands that stuck to her red face. There were big, wet circles on her dress under her armpits. When it got hot enough, she would head for the shade of the willow tree behind the house. She'd sit in one of the ragged wicker chairs under the tree and fan herself with a folded newspaper.

Lots of times she'd tell me to come out with her to get out of the heat. I already said she wasn't mean. It's just that, as I said, she never made me one of the family, even though she told everybody that she and Mr. Dobbs adopted me. Sometimes I thought she treated me like I was a pet monkey or something. The bad thing was that sitting out there in the shade away from the hot kitchen made me drowsy. But there was no sleeping. There was always the steaming kitchen, the tubs of boiling water, and more beans and tomatoes and peas waiting to be canned. I was counting the days until the first Monday after Labor Day.

Labor Day was still two weeks away when Mr. Dobbs came home from work and called me out to the chairs under the willow. I was scared at first. He never called me aside to talk unless I was to get a scolding. But he was smiling as I walked out there, and he patted the wicker chair next to him, telling me to have a seat.

"Mrs. Dobbs tells me you're doing a fine job with the canning, Carrie," he said. I relaxed a little and told him thank you. Maybe Mrs. Dobbs had told him about the report card, and he was going tell me I was doing a fine job at school, too.

"You're a great help to Mrs. Dobbs, and we both appreciate that. You can see what a lot of work there is to do around here," he said.

"Yes sir."

"Too much for one person to have to do alone."

"Oh yes, sir. I can surely see that."

I had no inkling of where this was leading, and finally he said, "You've done well in school, too." I smiled big, and I thought I knew what was coming next, but he went on and on, without ever getting back to my report card. In a little while, as he continued to talk, I felt that heaviness in my chest that I'd felt when Waverly left to join the army. I could only take in part of what he said.

"We've been pleased with...and I'm sure you can understand how an extra person in the house creates more...but of course we were more than happy to take you in as an act of kindness...and since it's not really necessary for a woman to have an abundance of education... no more school...keeping you out to help with the chores..."

Finally he said I was a good girl, and then he quit talking. I don't know what made him think he had to add that last part.

To: Mr. and Mrs. William Van Patten, New York, New York
From: Miss Louisa Van Patten, Bryn Mawr, Pennsylvania
August 5, 1917

Dear Mother and Father,

Your recent letter lifted my heart and made it soar with hap-
piness if for no other reason than to see your dear handwriting,
Father, and your sweet salutation and signature, Mother.

I'm sorry to hear that you are still upset about my decision to
stay here and enroll in the summer semester. However, I have some
good news that I hope will lift your spirits. My senior thesis, which I
have titled "The Mind of a Deviant Woman," has been accepted for
publication by the American Medical Association! It will appear in
the magazine *Hygeia.*

My professor, Dr. Armstrong, encouraged me to submit it. That
he would consider my work worthy of being submitted was flattering enough. I had not the slightest inclination that it would be
accepted!

Although I know you have both expressed concerns that my research would take me among lunatics, epileptics, and other deviants, I do so want you to know how much the work means to me.
Also it is my hope that you will see how the study of such misfits
is important for the advancement of our society, particularly if we
can rid the world of such deviants in a humane manner. My own
research has been confined to the female gender because of the
need to narrow my field, but I can assure you that work in a much
broader area is also being conducted.

You have pressed it upon me continually that this work, if it is
worthy at all, is unfit for a woman. I hope you can somehow see
that it is woman who is most likely to care about the future of our
human race since she is the mother and caretaker.

Mother, you, who are such an admirably loving and nurturing

caretaker, I believe will come closest to understanding my passion for an education and future course. It is my prayer that you will lead my dear, dear father, who is your wise, loving, and devoted husband, to some understanding.

You will both be happy to hear that Lemuel came down from New York last week to visit with me. It was a most pleasant and enjoyable visit. Mrs. Carson, my housemother and a dear soul, gave me permission to have dinner with him in town. I was pleased that she allowed it since Lemuel had dared to leave his busy position at the law firm in Richmond and would have been gravely disappointed had we not been able to see each other, as I would have been, of course. Truthfully, it didn't take a great deal of persuading for Mrs. Carson to allow it. She is so taken by his good looks and charm that I believe she is a little bit in love with him herself!

The other news is that I have been invited to Long Island for dinner at the home of Dr. Estabrook; you will remember him as the man I assisted in research last year. The research involved families in which feeblemindedness and immoral tendencies appear hereditary. He has read my paper and was impressed by it enough to ask me to attend the dinner, along with other notables in our field of interest. Further good news is that being on Long Island will give me the opportunity to come home to Manhattan for a visit with you.

The dinner is scheduled for the sixteenth. My plan is to arrive in Manhattan on the fourteenth and return to Bryn Mawr on the seventeenth. I hope the schedule will be agreeable to you because I do so look forward to coming home to see you. If you don't expect to be home at that time, please tell Hattie and Milton to expect me. I will, as you know, be perfectly safe with those two loyal servants even if you aren't there.

I send you all my love, dear Mother and Father.

Your loving daughter,
Louisa

5

LOUISA

The Estabrook home at Cold Spring Harbor on Long Island was, by Van Patten standards, decidedly modest, but Louisa could not have been more excited to accept their invitation to dinner if it had come from Governor Whitman himself.

Arthur Estabrook was a young scientist who had already made a name for himself at the Carnegie Institute of Washington, studying genetics and the laws of heredity, especially in regard to feeble-mindedness and insanity. Louisa had felt privileged to assist him at one point, if only in a minor way. It was Dr. Estabrook who had introduced her to the idea of eugenics—the sterilization of deviants to prohibit procreation of their kind.

Other than to express his dismay at the need to associate with the insane, Louisa's father had shown little interest in her field of study. However, he had certainly been distressed at the idea of her attending a dinner unescorted. Her mother was completely distraught, although the Estabrooks apparently hadn't given it a second thought. It had only made matters worse to remind her parents that if the dawning of the twentieth century almost two decades ago hadn't changed conventions, the Great War certainly had. Her father had insisted she not take a taxi alone to Long Island but that she allow Laurence, his chauffeur, to drive her to the gathering and wait for her.

Now that she was in the Estabrook parlor waiting for the call for dinner, she had to admit she did, in fact, feel a little awkward. It wasn't that she'd been left alone since she arrived. She'd received plenty of attention, but she couldn't help feeling that she was more of a curiosity than an equal of the other guests, since, besides being a female researcher, she was considerably younger than all of them.

"Excuse me." The sound of the voice momentarily startled her, and she turned to see the face of a young man. It was a pleasant enough face, but a bit too thin to be considered handsome. Dark eyes that hid something—sadness?—punctuated his face. A mouth that appeared hardened by intelligence smiled at her. "May I fetch you a glass of wine while we wait for dinner?" he asked.

She nodded and murmured a thank you. He moved away a few steps and took a glass from a waiter's tray. The waiter's appearance made it obvious that he had been sent over by an agency. Dr. Estabrook likely would not have been able to afford full-time help. The young man spoke again as he handed her the drink.

"You are Miss Louisa Van Patten, no doubt."

"I am," she said, "but—"

"But how did I know? It's quite clear that you are the only one here young enough to be Louisa Van Patten, the much-talked-about author of the paper published in that new American Medical Association magazine. 'The Mind of a Deviant Woman,' I believe."

"You've read it?"

"I have, and I found it quite interesting."

"Interesting? Safe answer. No commitment. No embarrassment."

"I'm not trying to be safe or save either of us from embarrassment," he said cordially. "I meant that I found the article interesting."

"I'm afraid you have me at a disadvantage," she said. "You know my name, but I don't know yours."

"Ben Newman."

"Are you an associate of Dr. Estabrook?"

"I'm a journalist. I work for a newspaper."

"A journalist..."

"You're wondering why I'm here among all of you intellectuals."

"Well, I—"

"Don't worry. Your inquisitiveness doesn't bother me. I'm inquisitive myself, as you might guess. And to answer your question, I've interviewed Dr. Estabrook several times for an article I'm writing on the eugenics movement. I must have impressed him. He invited me to his party. Now, tell me, how do you know Dr. Estabrook?"

"I'm a great admirer of his work in eugenics, and I did some work for him in his studies of hereditary traits of feeblemindedness. It was mostly clerical—tabulating statistics. I don't think he remembered me until that paper you mentioned was published. It's made me a bit of a curiosity."

He laughed. "You're a curiosity?"

"People still find it curious that a woman is interested in things like deviant minds. When I first arrived, Dr. Estabrook introduced me as 'one of our emerging generation whose little paper has revealed promise.' A little off-putting, wouldn't you say?"

He looked at her over the rim of his glass. "But you admire him—his work at least."

"Of course. As do you, I'm sure."

His eyes held hers for a beat before he responded. "Eugenics. The science of improving the human race through careful selection. Get rid of all the bad traits, and who is to decide what's bad?"

"I should think you know what the bad traits are." She was surprised at his sarcasm.

"Am I the one who gets to decide?"

"I'm afraid I don't understand what you're getting at," Louisa said. "Surely you understand the important implications of Dr. Estabrook's work."

"Oh yes, of course" There was a coldness in his eyes as he spoke. "The implication is that we aim to develop a master race, free of all imperfections. Your paper seems to argue that premise."

"Do I detect a note of sarcasm? Do you believe eugenics is harmful to society?"

Ben shrugged. "I'm a journalist. I'm supposed to remain objective, not make judgments."

Louisa gave him a look of amused wariness. "Ah, but you do make judgments, don't you?"

"I would never do that, Louisa. I'm the epitome of the ethical journalist."

She laughed and wished she had a clever comeback, but none was forthcoming. However, she was literally saved by the bell—a delicate crystal instrument shaken vigorously by a servant who announced that the guests were to be seated for dinner.

Ben held her arm lightly and escorted her into the dining room. The room was barely large enough to hold all of the guests, but the table had been laid prettily with decent china and a large, lovely floral arrangement in the center. A display of flickering candles on the table gave the room a feeling of civilized warmth.

While the waiter who had served the drinks was busy at a sideboard, another of his colleagues helped guests find the place cards that marked each one's proper seat at the table. Louisa was disappointed that she wasn't seated next to Ben until she noticed that the name on the card next to her was Mrs. Margaret Sanger.

Louisa's eyes widened, and for a moment she felt giddy. She hadn't spotted Mrs. Sanger in the crowded gathering before the guests were seated. She was one of the most controversial women in the country, and Louisa didn't know whether to admire or distrust her for her radical views. The woman had been tried for indecency for writing in shocking detail about birth control for women. Louisa had no doubt that birth control was to a woman's advantage, especially for the poor, uneducated class, but to write about it in such graphic terms with descriptions of conception, no matter how scientific and clinical, was another matter. Indecent? Louisa wasn't sure. Perhaps it was only that it was unfamiliar. Most shocking of all, however, was that Mrs. Sanger supported sexual relationships outside of marriage, and it was said that she took lovers even though she was married. Free love, it was called.

Ben found his place at the table directly across from Louisa. He gave her a smile as he pulled out his chair. "At least I'm guaranteed a pleasant view as I dine, but I hope we won't have to shout at each other to be heard."

Before Louisa could respond, Ben rose from his chair and gave a nod to the small, pretty woman who had come to take a seat next to her. The woman, who was obviously Margaret Sanger, had to pull out her own chair. She managed with considerable grace and returned a cordial nod to Ben.

The seating arrangement was certainly unorthodox, Louisa noted. Her mother would be appalled at an informal plan that deviated from the traditional male, female, male, female pattern. Mrs. Sanger showed no sign of being bothered by it, however. She turned to Louisa and spoke to her in a voice that Louisa found surprisingly soft, given her reputation for fierceness.

"I don't believe we had a chance to meet during the cocktail hour," she said. "I'm Mrs. Margaret Sanger."

"Oh yes, Mrs. Sanger, I know who you are. I'm Louisa Van Patten." She knew Mrs. Sanger only by reputation, and although photographs of her had appeared in newspapers and other publications many times, Louisa wasn't certain she would have recognized her. The photos had depicted a pleasant enough face, but Mrs. Sanger was much prettier in person. Her perfectly smooth skin was fair with a golden tint. Her large, expressive dark eyes were set above high cheekbones, giving her a classic look. Her face was perfectly framed by shining dark hair styled in the new bob. She wore a simple black satin dress with a long string of pearls looping across her small bosom. Louisa had heard the stories of how Mrs. Sanger had come from Irish immigrant stock, but her simple and elegant beauty could compete in the most aristocratic of circles.

"Miss Van Patten," Mrs. Sanger said, "I've heard of you as well. Mr. Eastabrook speaks so highly of you and the impressive paper you wrote for *Hygeia*."

Louisa felt herself blushing, and she wasn't certain how to reply. Mrs. Sanger continued talking, however, putting her at ease.

"I'm going to have to confess up front that I haven't read your paper, which I know doesn't speak very highly of me, but it's better

I embarrass myself now rather than later by trying to make you think I have. I hope you're not offended."

"Of course I'm not offended, Mrs. Sanger. I'm pleased you've even heard of it."

"Please call me Margaret. And of course I've heard of it. It's all the talk among the eugenicists. And I can assure you I have every intention of reading it." She laughed, a pleasant throaty sound. "How many times have you heard *that* platitude?"

"Not often at all," Louisa said, "since that's the only paper I've ever published."

"I understand that it's a comprehensive study of mentally deficient women."

"I hesitate to call it comprehensive," Louisa said. "I feel I have a great deal more work to do on the subject, but yes, I've at least introduced the beginnings of a look into the minds of deviants."

"Any conclusions?" Margaret asked.

"Well, it does appear to me that intellectual deviancy and moral deviancy go hand in hand," Louisa said. She was pleased with the attention but enough in awe of the woman to worry that she might come across as naive or, worse, unintelligent.

"Morally deficient?" Margaret asked.

"Prostitutes are often feebleminded, I believe."

"Some say that women are forced into prostitution by their circumstances. They would choose something else if they could."

"If they could. That's the point, isn't it?" Louisa said. "Are they unable to find a way out because they are feebleminded or for some other reason? I'm not making a moral judgment, Margaret. I'm conducting a study of the minds of all kinds of deviants, including epileptics, morons, and imbeciles, and I consider the paper no more than a tiny crack in a door that needs to be opened widely."

"And you plan to do that, Miss Van Patten? Open that door wider, I mean."

"If I'm to call you Margaret, then you must call me Louisa," she said with a little laugh. "And yes, I do plan to do that. I'm in the process of looking for subjects for my study."

"Good for you, Louisa!" Margaret managed to say that without sounding patronizing, surprising Louisa with her response. "I'm a great supporter of the eugenics movement—the betterment of the human race through birth control, including sterilization of the unfit. The financial and cultural costs of these classes to the community are enormous."

"Yes, of course they are." Louisa felt relieved. She saw now that Margaret had been merely testing her with her earlier response about prostitutes.

"If we somehow winnowed out these people, think of the funds that would be available for human development, for scientific, artistic, and philosophic research!" Margaret's eyes were luminous and her face animated as she leaned forward and gently slapped the table with one of her long, white hands. "Why there would be hundreds of millions of dollars available that we now have to spend on the care and segregation of these people who never should have been born."

"Oh, Mrs. . . .I mean, Margaret, I do agree most enthusiastically," Louisa said. "It is the future of the human race we speak of!"

"Forgive me. . ." The words came from Ben, speaking from across the table. He was leaning forward, looking at both of them. "Forgive me, but I couldn't help overhearing your conversation."

"Of course we forgive you," Margret said with a slight laugh that sounded flirtatious.

"I wonder; who gets the privilege of determining just who the unfit are?" Ben was smiling as he spoke, but it was cordial rather than flirtatious.

Margaret's smile faded. "Oh. . ." She sounded crestfallen. "You are no doubt among those who advocate benevolent charities for the feebleminded and epileptic and the like."

"'The cruelty of charity' is the way you've described it in your writings, I believe."

"I'm pleased you've read my work," she said, "and yes, I consider philanthropy and charity emotional and altruistic ways of meeting nothing more than individual situations of human defect and dependence. They are concerned with symptoms and cannot strike at the radical causes of social misery."

"Cannot?" Ben asked.

"Charities are sentimental and paternalistic." She paused briefly. "Please, sir, I don't believe I've heard your name."

"The name is Newman, Ben Newman, and, just for the record, I have no affiliation with any charity."

"Forgive me," she said with a smile. "Your question was so pointed, I thought—"

"My question is simplistic more than pointed. Simplistic and sincere. Who decides who is unfit?"

"Mr. Newman, morons, idiots, epileptics, and prostitutes, I'm sure you'll agree, are not difficult for even the uneducated to recognize." Margaret's voice had grown decidedly colder.

"I'm not certain I do agree, Madam," Ben said.

"What do you propose then? Some sort of test?"

"Perhaps. If it protects—"

"A waste of public money," Margaret said, cutting Ben off in midsentence. "There are instances when common sense would suffice."

"I'm sure you're right," Ben said, "but I don't believe this is one of them."

"Surely you can see the advantage to society of remodeling the human race to higher intelligence through the management of heredity? It's the only way civilization can live up to its name. By that, I mean only thus can we create bodies that are a fitting temple for the soul."

"Create a super race, you mean?"

Margaret nodded. "For the entire human race. I should think you would see the advantage in that."

Ben leaned a little closer as he spoke to her from across the table. "I do indeed, but I also see the disadvantage of the process."

"Yes, as you mentioned." She smiled again, perhaps a little condescendingly. "I believe you can rest assured that your concerns are ill-founded."

Ben returned her smile with equal condescendence. "Let's hope you're right."

"Indeed." She turned her attention to her salad without looking up. For the rest of the meal, she spoke to Louisa and others around her without engaging Ben.

When the dinner was over, Ben sought out Louisa. "May I offer you a ride home?" he asked.

"Thank you, but my father's driver is waiting for me," she said, "and it's a long ride. All the way to Manhattan."

He shrugged. "Doesn't hurt to ask."

She studied his face. "You're in a hurry to leave. I don't think you enjoyed the evening, did you?"

"Parts of it."

"Why were you goading Mrs. Sanger?"

"Goading?" He laughed. "I wasn't goading. I was questioning her."

"So you said—simple and sincere questions. But you certainly didn't come across as objective. And I suspect you knew what her answers would be before you asked."

He shrugged and grinned. "I did more or less know her answers. I've read much of what she's written."

"You simply wanted to argue, I suppose."

"I don't like arguments. I hoped she could justify her position."

"And she did."

"And she did not."

Louisa frowned. "But surely you can see—"

"Look, if we're going to talk about this, can't we at least go some-place comfortable?" He took her arm. "Send your driver home, and I'll take you to a quiet little place where we can have a cocktail and talk. And I'll take you home afterward," he added. "Your company will be worth the long drive."

"Oh, but I couldn't."

"Why not? You're not married, are you?"

"No, but I have—"

"Look, I'm not asking you to run away with me. I just would like to talk more with the woman who wrote 'The Mind of a Deviant Woman.' I promise I won't try to seduce you."

Louisa laughed, albeit a little uneasily. "Of course I would enjoy talking to you, and of course you're trying to seduce me by telling me you want to talk about my work. We can just stay here though, and—"

"Do you really want to stay here?"

She paused, looking around at the crowd of guests. "Well..."

"That's what I thought," he said, taking her arm and leading her toward the exit.

It wasn't easy to persuade her father's dismayed driver that she wouldn't need him to drive her home, but once it was done and she found herself in a quiet lounge sipping a cocktail with Ben, she soon forgot about the worried driver.

Although Ben seemed to have a genuine interest in her work, it didn't occur to her until later that a good part of the evening was spent laughing and talking of far more trivial matters, drinking more than her usual limit of one cocktail, and even allowing Ben to show her a new dance step called the foxtrot.

Neither did it occur to her until she was at home in her bed that she had not thought of Lemuel even once during the evening.

6

J. T.

A little breeze had come up causing the willow to toss her long tresses flirtatiously, the way a young woman might when she's trying to attract a lover. J. T. had, at some point in the past, thought of young women's hair when he looked at the willow. Now, however, his only thoughts were to acknowledge the sense of self-satisfaction that surrounded him.

The girl had taken the news well. She'd always been what you might call docile and had always seemed properly grateful to him for giving her a home. Not at all like Lucy—he chuckled when he thought of her—high spirited, not afraid to let everybody know what she thought or what she wanted. He'd worried for a while that she would never be able to put a damper on it long enough to find a husband, but she found somebody, and he was grateful.

Even so, that feistiness was good for a girl like Lucy. It just meant she'd always come out on top if she set her mind to it. It was different with Carrie though. She was better off keeping her demands and opinions to herself. She was better off being what he would call, well, obedient.

It wasn't that she was dumb. She was smart enough to know what she came from and how much better off she was than if she'd been raised by that whorin' mother of hers. Old Emma Buck—now there was a case for you. He had lost count of the times he'd arrested her for loitering or, worse, for prostitution. Must have been half a dozen times or more over the years, maybe twice that. One time—what was it, maybe six years ago? She had a little girl with her. She was drunk and out trying to turn a trick. Made Judge Shackelford madder than a wet hen when she was brought before him, and J. T. gave him the facts.

Shackelford was a young man then, just beginning to learn the judging business. Full of righteousness and a crusading spirit. Threw Emma in jail till she sobered up and then asked J. T., "Why don't you take the child?"

"Why, I can't do that, Judge. I got a family of my own," he told him.

"So you do, J. T.," the judge said, "and I'm sure the time will come when Alice will need some help around the house."

Well now, J. T. hadn't thought of that. But the judge was right; it would be nice to have some help around the house, and that little girl would grow up before you knew it. Alice would appreciate it; he was sure. She always wanted him to hire somebody to help her out, but that was something he couldn't afford on a peace officer's salary.

"Besides the help she will eventually provide, it will be an act of kindness toward her on your part, J. T."

Those words were barely out of the judge's mouth before J. T. agreed to do it.

Now, as he sat beneath the swaying fronds of the willow with a light breeze to refresh him, he thought that things couldn't have turned out better. He'd held on to a good job for years now and had even managed to buy a little house. He had a son and a daughter, respect and standing in the community, and now household help. Life was good for J. T. Dobbs. He fell asleep basking in his contentment, but within a few minutes he was awakened by his wife telling him to go see what he could do with Carrie. She'd locked herself in her room.

Wouldn't you know it? Just when he was getting comfortable. A person would think he could get some peace when he got home, especially since he did this all day—going to see about somebody making trouble. If it wasn't a vagrant or a prostitute or a drunk, it was his own household.

"Carrie! Didn't you hear me knock? Open the door. Now! What are you doing in there, anyway? Carrie!"

He was breathing hard from the exertion of getting his corpulent frame up out of the wicker chair and hurrying to get inside. Maybe a little bit from anger as well.

He knocked again, harder this time.

"Don't knock the door down, J. T.!"

He turned to look at Alice with a scowl on his face. He was in no mood for instructions. But he didn't say anything. No point in getting into an argument. That would only make it longer before he could get back to his rest. He turned back to the door, knocked on it—with more restraint this time—and swore under his breath.

"What did you say, J. T.? Was that a swear word you used?"

J. T. ignored his wife's question and addressed Carrie instead. "I said get yourself out of that room and talk to me!"

"No" came a tiny voice from behind the door.

J. T.'s eyes widened. "Don't tell me no. Now come on out of there."

"I can't." Her two words lacked force and could only seep toward him from under the door.

"Of course you can." J. T. was finding it harder by the minute to conceal his anger. "Now open this door! You should be in the kitchen helping Mrs. Dobbs get supper on the table. We all have to earn our keep around here!"

He heard something—a shuffling or shifting—but no words. Perhaps a different tactic would work. "Carrie?" He tried to force his voice to gentleness. "Won't you tell me what's wrong?"

"Don't mollycoddle her! We can't let her get by with that." Alice's voice creaked with disgust.

J. T. wished she'd go back to the kitchen. If he had his way, he'd just leave Carrie in there so he could get back to that wicker chair. He'd figured out by now that she must not have taken his news about not going back to school so well after all. Now she was sulking about it. He had to admit Alice was right though. If he let her get away with it once, it would happen over and over.

After a resigned sigh, he started to knock again, but his knuckles had not met the door when it opened and Carrie was standing in the doorway.

She didn't speak. She simply glanced first at J. T. and then at Alice, and then she walked up the hall to the kitchen. J. T. saw that her eyes were red and swollen and knew she'd been crying.

Alice caught his eye and seemed as bewildered as he was.

"What did you say to her that made her go to her room and pout like that?" Alice asked.

"I told her just what you told me to tell her," J. T. said. He knew it sounded defensive, but he often felt he had to defend himself against Alice.

"About her not going back to school? That wasn't just my idea. You brought it up a long time ago. I only pointed out that now was the time."

"Now, Alice, let's not try to place blame," J. T. said, seizing the opportunity to appear the nobler of the two. "We can allow her a little time to get used to the idea. Everything will turn out just fine; you'll see."

Alice gave him a little snort in reply and turned away to join Carrie in the kitchen. By now J. T. could see no point in going back to the wicker chair. It would be difficult to recapture his relaxed mood, and the mosquitoes liked the shade the willow provided this time of day. If he went to the living room, he'd be sure to feel the tension coming from the kitchen. There was nothing to do but leave. A short walk, maybe. It would clear his head and help him get rid of the disgruntled feeling the women of his household often left him with.

He walked out of the house and headed south with no particular thought or intention of a destination, but he was headed toward the intersection of Market and Main, the center of town, the center of activity. It was where he spent most of his working day and, in fact, most of his life. He'd had his job as one of Charlottesville's peace officers for almost five years now. Before that he'd worked for the railroad, even made it to foreman of the labor section. His peace officer job was much more to his liking. It put him in touch with the public, made him recognizable by most people in the town, and made him feel as if he had his finger on the pulse of Charlottesville's life and activity—not just the seamy underbelly but the town's politics as well. Alice had encouraged him to take the job, although she cared little for public recognition or the politics and personalities of the town's elite. It was the money that interested her. And rightly so, he thought. They'd had two kids to raise and Alice's widowed mother and younger sister living with them, at least a while, until her mother died and her sister went off to live on her own. Matilda, her sister, never married. Strange woman, J. T. thought. At one time he thought she might be feebleminded, but she'd proved to be smart enough to make her own living. Still, a woman who preferred to live on her own without a man didn't seem quite right.

J. T. knew that everybody who knew Alice considered her a good woman, and he couldn't deny that she was. They'd come through a lot of bad times together, including the death of two children as well as some pretty lean times. Alice was the strong one—the one who always kept them going. Even when the babies died, and that was harder on her than anything else they'd been through. He couldn't blame her for putting extra pressure on him recently to take Carrie out of school. Sure, he'd accused her of nagging him, but when he thought about it, he could see how she deserved the full-time help Carrie would provide. Beyond that, he'd promised Alice from the beginning, when he was trying to convince her to take Carrie in, that she would one day be full-time help.

It was just that he had dreaded telling Carrie. He knew how much she liked going to school, and besides that, she was a good kid. He hated to disappoint her. Then, just when he'd thought things had gone smoothly, Carrie had her little fit and locked herself in the bedroom. Oh well, it was over and done with now, and nobody seemed any worse for it. Carrie would get over it. He could see that now. Females always had to take a little time to pout when things didn't go their way. Even Alice was always sulking about something he did or failed to do.

This little walk had been good for him, given him a chance to think things through. He didn't expect he'd have to worry about Carrie anymore.

"Hey there, J. T." The voice and the sound of his name spoken in such a familiar tone startled him at first. When he looked up, he saw that it was Emma Buck who had spoken to him. Her two brats weren't with her this time. Maybe she'd done them a favor and put them in an orphanage.

He mumbled her name as a way of greeting and looked for a way to move away from her. They were standing in front of the pool hall on Market Street—Emma's territory—and J. T. wondered what in hell had made him come this way. He could have just as easily walked the opposite direction toward the river.

"My girl doin' all right?" she asked.

"Just fine."

"Well, she looked good that last time I seen her."

"Yes ma'am." He moved his gaze beyond her a moment, looking for a way to escape.

She laughed. Was she laughing at him for being uncomfortable? At the same time, her breath wafted a familiar smell.

"You been drinking, Emma?"

"What if I have? It ain't no crime."

"Where're your kids?" he asked, slipping into his professional role.

"Right now at the orphanage. Just temporary. Just till I get on my feet." She looked at the ground, suddenly unwilling to meet his eyes with her defiant look.

"On your back, you mean?"

She laughed, sending out another blast of alcohol-laden breath. "Never figured you had a sense of humor, J. T."

"I ain't trying to be funny, Emma."

"No, I guess you wouldn't, would you?" The defiance was back.

"You been drinking?" he asked again.

"No."

The blatant lie irritated him. "You can't take care o' your kids, but you can buy liquor."

"It ain't your place to preach to me, J. T."

"Somebody ought to take them kids away from you," J. T. said.

Emma curled her lip in a derisive smile. "You offering to take 'em?"

Her quick retort angered him. "Don't get smart with me, whore. You ought to be locked up somewhere, and I'm the man who can do it."

She studied his face for a moment, still with the impertinent smile on her lips. J. T. was caught by her eyes. No smile there. No alcoholic haze. Just two gray stones polished with something that frightened him. A dangerous shrewdness maybe.

She turned and walked away from him, laughing.

From: C. D. Shackelford, Justice of the Peace, Albemarle County, Virginia
To: J.T. Dobbs, Peace Officer, Charlottesville, Virginia
November 10, 1918

Dear J. T.,

I am in receipt of your recent letter regarding one Emma Buck of Charlottesville. I seem to recall receiving a similar letter a year or so ago, which I passed on to Mrs. Anne Harris, the district nurse. You have informed me of your frustration in dealing with what you have referred to as "too much red tape and passing the buck" after Mrs. Harris failed to respond. Therefore, I have resolved to clear up this matter myself since you are a valued employee of the city. I will contact Mrs. Harris personally.

You will understand, of course, that my decision in no way reflects a lack of confidence in Nurse Harris. I can assure you her delay was only because she was trying to follow prescribed procedure, although I can see how those who have no knowledge of the mechanics of government could interpret it as what you refer to as "the runaround."

You have expressed frustration with your efforts to have Mrs. Buck incarcerated for deviancy, including drunkenness and immoral soliciting, only to have her released within a day each time. I can assure you that I, as well as Nurse Harris, share your desire to rid the streets of our beloved Charlottesville of the likes of Mrs. Buck on a permanent basis.

In light of that, I must ask you if you have ever had cause to believe that Mrs. Buck might be feebleminded.? Does she seem unwilling to care for or incapable of caring for herself or her children? (I am aware, of course, that one of them has been placed in your home for care, and as I recall, it was precisely because her mother was unable to care for her properly.) Does Mrs. Buck seem incapable of carrying out simple instructions? For example, have you instructed her to stop drinking and to cease her immoral solicitations, and she has not followed through?

If you feel the case fits any of these criteria, I suggest that you come to my office to complete and sign papers requesting to have her examined by physicians who will determine her mental capacity. Should you decide to do that, you will be instructed to escort Mrs. Buck to the courthouse for a hearing at which I will preside. At that time, physicians will examine her, and if a suitable conclusion is reached, she will be placed in the Virginia State Colony for Epileptics and Feebleminded.

Sincerely,
C. D. Shackelford
Justice of the Peace

7

CARRIE

I was in the kitchen holding two chickens by their feet. I had just killed and plucked them and cleaned out their guts and other organs. Now I had to burn the pin feathers off by holding them over a stove burner. I was just about to do that when I heard Mr. Dobbs speak.

"They ain't going to do a damn thing about old Emma," he said.

Naturally that got my attention. I knew he was talking about Mama. Then I heard Mrs. Dobbs tell him to watch his language because this was a Christian household. If I went ahead and singed the pin feathers, they would smell it since there's nothing else that stinks like burned chicken feathers. That would make them leave the room, maybe go outside. I wanted them to stay where I could hear more.

Mr. Dobbs cleared his throat with a grumble like he always did when he was angry. "Well, I done all I could. Wrote to the county nurse and Judge Shackelford both and went and signed them damn papers, but not a thing has happened. That's the gov'ment for you."

"Well, I wish they'd put Emma away as much as you do. I just don't like the way Carrie acts when she's around her mama." Mrs. Dobbs always spoke in a round voice that came up from her stomach, which was just as round. "I seen her give her mama money once, but I put a stop to that. Gave Carrie a good swat and wouldn't let her see her friends for two days."

"She give her money? Where's she gettin' any money?"

"I let her keep a quarter ever' once in a while when I hire her out to somebody."

Another grumble. "Well, I'll be damned. Give her a quarter, and she gives it to that woman to spend on liquor."

"I wish you wouldn't swear like that, and anyway, I told you I put a stop to it, so just hush your mouth about it," Mrs. Dobbs said.

Mr. Dobbs growled something I couldn't understand, but I heard the rocking chair squeak as Mrs. Dobbs stood up. I knew that meant she'd be in the kitchen soon, so I went to the stove, stoked up the fire under a front burner, and held one of the chickens over the flame while the other chicken rested in a dishpan full of cool water.

I wished I could tell Mr. Dobbs I didn't give Mama money to spend on liquor. I gave it to her because she's my mama and because Doris and Roy are my brother and sister. I guess I liked to think of them as my family because, like I said before, nobody, not even the Dobbses, thought of me as a part of their family.

I never said a word when Mrs. Dobbs came in the kitchen. She didn't say anything either. She just went over to the flour bin and took some out to make biscuits. She started humming "Jesus Calls Us," low and singsongy, the way she did sometimes when she was cooking.

Mr. Dobbs passed through the kitchen on his way out to the chair under the willow tree. The only thing he said was "Ain't nothin' I hate worse than the smell of singed pin feathers."

It was several days later before I saw Mama again. I was on my way to Sparks Grocery and General Merchandise to buy some things for Mrs. Dobbs. Mama was standing half a block away, leaning against the window of the pool hall and smoking a cigarette. I waved to her and called out to her to wait there until I got done with the shopping. While I was in there, I used my own money to buy a loaf of bread for Mama and the kids and a packet of hair ribbons for Doris. Now, no one could accuse me of giving my mother money for liquor.

"Give the ribbons to Doris next time you see her," I told her, "and tell Roy I'll buy him something next time."

That's when Mama said, "Thank you, hon; you're a real angel." Well, that got me. She never had called me "hon" before, or angel, or any other of the sweet names I'd heard other mothers use. I wanted that moment to last forever. I wanted to stay there, taking in that moist smell that was my mother, but then she saw a man across the street staring at her. She waved to him and ambled toward him with the loaf of bread under her arm, leaving me behind. There wasn't anything for me to do except go back to the Dobbses' house with the groceries. I ran all the way.

I saw her one more time that summer. Me and Winona Sparks and Lottie Vernon were in the grocery store when Mama came in. She didn't seem like she saw me, or maybe she just pretended not to. I didn't make any effort to get her attention. I told myself it wasn't that I would be embarrassed to talk to her with my friends around. If that wasn't it, though, I can't think of any other reason.

I stayed awake until well past midnight that night just feeling so bad because the truth was that I really *was* embarrassed that Emma Buck was my mother.

Then Labor Day came and went, and everybody but me was back in school. I tried not to think about it. I just kind of let it dry up like the flowers Lucy used to put between the pages of books. She just let them stay there until all of the color was gone and there was nothing but sort of an outline of what they used to be.

I felt so lonesome sometimes I thought I would cry. I missed Waverly even more than my friends from school. He wrote letters a few times to Mr. and Mrs. Dobbs, but I wasn't allowed to read them. The best I could do was listen in when Mrs. Dobbs told someone that Waverly was in France, but he seemed to be doing fine. At least nobody had shot him, she'd always say.

Lucy and Tom were living in Lovingston, and Lucy was expecting another baby soon. I didn't miss her as much as I did Waverly. It surprised me that I did miss her a little though. I missed the sound of her voice at night when I went into our room. It wasn't that we ever talked since Lucy did all of the talking, mostly about herself, but at least it was a human sound and kept things from being so lonely. At least I had Annabelle.

I hardly ever saw my old friends once school started, except for seeing Winona Sparks a few times at the grocery store her daddy owned.

Winona would always speak to me first. She'd say hi and ask me how I was doing. I always told her I was doing just fine.

"Well, I'm not," she told me one day. "I got the curse."

"What curse?" I asked.

"You know, the visit from Aunt Flow."

"Who?"

"Good Lord, Carrie, you don't even know what I'm talking about!" She sounded kind of disgusted when she said that, and then she leaned closer to me and whispered, "I'm talking about menstruating."

"Oh," I said again. I knew what that meant. Lucy had told me about the monthly bleeding.

"It means I'm a woman now," Winona said. "It means I can have babies. Obviously, it hasn't happened to you." It sounded like she said that to make me feel bad. "It's messy and painful," she added.

"Painful?" Lucy had never said anything about that, although I noticed she got awful cranky when the monthlies rolled around.

Winona just laughed at me. "You'll see," she said and walked away toward the back of the store where customers weren't allowed. After that, I didn't see her much, and when I did see her, we didn't have much to talk about. I knew that she and all of the other girls were living in a different world from the one I was living in now, and theirs, I knew, was hundreds of times more interesting than mine.

From: Miss Louisa Van Patten, Bryn Mawr, Pennsylvania
To: Mrs. Anne Harris, District Nurse, Albemarle County, Virginia
November 1918

Dear Mrs. Harris,

I wanted to take this opportunity to tell you how inspired I was by the presentation you made to our sociology class last semester at Bryn Mawr. Your work among indigents in Albemarle County, Virginia, is most definitely admirable and courageous. I was particularly interested in the information you gave us regarding your assessment of deviant women and, in particular, one Emma Buck.

You may remember that I approached you after the class and told you of my interest in studying the minds of deviant women because I was preparing my senior thesis on the subject. At that time you very graciously invited me to come to Charlottesville sometime in the future to accompany you on your professional visits to Mrs. Buck.

As I mentioned during our encounter after class, I have collected a great deal of information on the subject of the minds of deviant women and have had the opportunity to interview some of the unfortunates. You may have even read the paper I submitted to the American Medical Association. I am now researching the subject for a book while I remain at Bryn Mawr doing graduate work. I am most anxious to include Mrs. Buck in my research and to observe your interactions with her. I am certain it will add greatly to my understanding of the subject and most certainly to the development of my book.

Will you be so kind as to inform me of a convenient time in the near future for me to come to Charlottesville? I can't express strongly enough how eager I am for this opportunity and for the opportunity to include your insights in my research.

Your most humble student,
Louisa Van Patten

8

CARRIE

The most exciting thing that happened to me after I was forced to drop out of school came about on the day Mrs. Dobbs rushed into the house with a kind of hurried wobble. That was the closest she ever came to running. She had been out to get the mail from the mailbox on the street. She was waving a letter in the air and screeching, "He's coming home! He's coming home!"

"Coming home?" I asked. "You mean Waverly? He's really coming home?"

"Yes, yes! Waverly! He's coming home from the war!" Mrs. Dobbs pulled me toward her in a big hug. That was only the second time in all the years I had lived with the Dobbses that she ever really hugged me, although she did pat me on the head fairly often. The first time I got a hug was when she found out Lucy was pregnant with her first child.

When Mr. Dobbs came home from work, he was just as happy as Mrs. Dobbs and I were, and he started talking about having a big party to celebrate Waverly's homecoming.

"The neighbors will be just as glad to see him as we are," he said, "and as many kin folks as we can get ahold of will want to see him, too."

I always liked having parties, even when I had to do most of the cooking and a lot of the work, but I wasn't too excited about this one. I really wanted Waverly just for us. Well, actually, just for me. At least Lucy wouldn't be around to take up his time since she was expecting a baby soon. I hoped that meant her friend Audrey wouldn't show up either.

"Lucy will just have to wait to see him." I was as surprised as anyone to hear myself saying that out loud. It was just that I was so excited I really didn't know what I was saying.

"What do you mean by that?" Mrs. Dobbs was frowning at me.

I felt myself blushing and feeling like she could read my mind. "Well, she's going to be having her baby any day now, so I guess she won't—"

Mrs. Dobbs laughed. "Oh Lordy, child, Lucy will have that baby long before Waverly gets here."

I couldn't quite make sense of what she was saying. "But isn't Waverly coming here when he—"

"He has to come all the way from France, Carrie. That's the other side of the ocean. That will take some time." Instead of sounding like she was scolding me, Mrs. Dobbs was smiling when she said that. The thought of Waverly coming home, no matter how long it might take, had put her in a good mood.

"Then he'll have to go through a bunch of red tape to get hisself taken out of the army," Mr. Dobbs said. "Could be weeks."

"Oh," I said. I didn't make any effort to hide my disappointment. I wouldn't let myself go on feeling that way though. At least he was coming home. He would be here with us—with me. And it wouldn't seem so lonesome anymore.

Time just seemed to drag by even though I did my best to keep busy. I had planted a garden that was ready to harvest. That meant starting the canning. I also cleaned the house from top to bottom, and of course there was always the cooking. I tired myself out completely every day just so I could go to sleep.

Finally, it was the day for Waverly to come home. He had sent a letter to us, telling us he would come from Newport News. He had bought a car, he said, and would be driving it home, and he was bringing a surprise. The surprise would be something special from France, I just knew, and I couldn't wait to see it.

Lucy and Tom got there first, and they brought their new little girl. She was the prettiest little thing I had ever seen. She had chubby little pink cheeks and the prettiest little mouth. I love babies, and I especially loved this one. I was hoping they had named her Annabelle, but it turned out they had named her Frances. If it had been any other time except the day Waverly was coming home, I could have spent the entire day holding her and looking at her. As it was, when I wasn't busy in the kitchen, I couldn't keep my eyes off of the front door or from shifting my gaze out to the side yard where Waverly would drive up in his new car.

As it turned out, several people got there early, including Mrs. Dobbs's sister with her husband and family, including Clarence the Pest. They were all talking and laughing in the living room while me and Mrs. Dobbs and our neighbor Mrs. Wells worked in the kitchen. Mrs. Dobbs and Mrs. Wells were peeling potatoes, and I was trying to pull out the big pot to put them in to boil. It was shoved back in the bottom of the cupboard, and I was making even more noise than the people in the living room as I moved other pots aside to get to the big one.

That's why I didn't hear Waverly's car or see him walking up to the door. It wasn't until I heard Lucy call his name that I knew he was there.

"Oh, Waverly! You're home. My baby brother is home!"

There was all kinds of racket after that, people laughing and talking, chairs scraping on the floor as they stood up to greet him, and Mrs. Dobbs squealing behind me. She almost pushed me down as she worked her way around me to get to Waverly. I knew it was Waverly. I knew he was really home because I recognized his voice as he greeted people and his laugh that meant he was as glad to see everyone as they were to see him.

I made my way out of the kitchen, and there he was! He had turned into a man. He was tall and muscular, although still thin, and his hair was shorter than I'd ever seen it before. He had just finished giving his aunt a hug when Lucy spoke.

"And who is *this*?" she asked.

I saw that she was looking at a young woman standing beside Waverly, and I heard his laugh again.

"This?" he said. "This is Mrs. Waverly Dobbs. We got married yesterday in Newport."

Everyone squealed and screeched and moved in even closer to Waverly and the woman beside him. I turned away and went back into the kitchen just in time to hear him add, "Me and Florence already rented a place in Newport, and I got a job at the shipyard."

He didn't notice when I went back to the kitchen—didn't even notice that I wasn't there to greet him.

To make matters worse, Clarence wouldn't leave me alone. He looked different from the last time I saw him. His face was covered with pimples, and he'd got to where he was real sullen all the time, but he was still just as annoying as he had always been. He tried to trip me several times when I carried dishes from the kitchen to the table in the dining room. Worst of all, he had grown a dirty mind. He kept saying vulgar things to me when he thought no one else could hear. It was things like "I see your titties are bigger than the last time I seen 'em. I can see 'em sticking out more. You got hair on your pussy, too?"

All I could do was tell him to shut up. I wasn't in the mood for putting up with anything. Knowing Waverly was married to that woman made me feel bad. Besides that, I had started to have an achy feeling low in my midsection that radiated down my legs, and I felt real sluggish. When I noticed the damp feeling between my legs, I asked to be excused from helping with the cooking and hurried to the outhouse.

The blood was no surprise. Winona had described everything. If what she said was true, I was a woman now. That was supposed to be the good part.

I wasn't certain there was anything good about being a woman. Well, maybe if you were Waverly's wife. For sure my mama hadn't got anything good from being a woman. She looked paler and more tired every time I saw her, and I was pretty sure she was drinking more.

I know it wasn't good to think about sad things like that all the time, and that's why I tried to concentrate on good things. But what was good about this awful cramping and this messy blood and this grumpy feeling I had? Nothing came to mind immediately. Maybe that was why they called it a curse.

Still, if what Winona and Lucy said was true, this was all part of what made it possible for women to have babies. That was good. I couldn't remember all of the details Lucy gave me—something about if you didn't have sex with a man to put a baby inside you, then blood comes out of your body. It didn't really make sense, but it was something like that.

Having babies was of no concern to me right then. I wasn't going to tell Mrs. Dobbs that my flow had come either, lest she caution me about the expense of buying those pads. I'd already bought a box of Kotex and an elastic belt to hold them in place. I used my own money, saved from the little bit I was allowed to keep when other women paid to have me help with their housework.

Putting on the pad took longer than I expected. I wasn't sure just how the pads were supposed to fit on that contraption the clerk had called a sanitary belt. The clerk was a young woman, and she was so embarrassed about having to sell the thing that she couldn't have told me how to use it even if she'd wanted to. I finally got it done, but the cramping low in my belly was getting worse.

When I got back to the kitchen, Mrs. Dobbs said, "Good Lord, Carrie, where you been? We got twenty souls here to feed, and you disappear." She was so busy stirring pots, pulling dishes from the cupboard, and peeking in the oven, I don't know how she even knew I'd been gone. All I could do was tell her I was sorry, but I had to go to the toilet. She looked at me funny, and I couldn't tell if she thought I was lying or what. All I know is it made me feel grumpy for her to look at me like that.

The next morning she came to my room before I got out of bed, which was something she hardly ever did because I was in the habit of getting up on my own—even without an alarm clock.

"Carrie! What's wrong with you? I hope you ain't sick," she said.

I was sound asleep until I heard her voice, and even then I had a hard time coming out of the fog. A twinge of cramping in my womb finally woke me up. Instead of jumping out of bed the way I usually did, I pulled the covers over my head and curled up.

Mrs. Dobbs started asking me again if I was sick, and she sounded worried. I was pretty sure her worry wasn't about me, but about me not being able to work. I was feeling grumpier than ever, so I told her to go away and leave me alone.

"Don't you talk to me that way!" she said. I didn't say anything, and I didn't uncurl myself. So she said, "I'm going to have to tell Mr. Dobbs about this."

"So tell him," I said from under the covers.

Well, Mrs. Dobbs got mad and stomped out of the room. I knew I'd cooked my goose with that back talk, so I threw back the covers and got dressed. I was in the kitchen in less than fifteen minutes cooking breakfast, but I didn't feel like talking to anybody. I heard Mrs. Dobbs murmuring to Lucy, who had spent the night there with her husband, that she never could stand a sulky child, and that I was crazy if I thought she was going to put up with this.

That just made me feel even more sullen. I didn't care though. I didn't care about anything. Until the third day when the cramps finally went away.

9

LOUISA

Louisa Van Patten was nervous about accompanying Anne Harris on her rounds to visit indigent clients—or should she call them patients? She wasn't sure she'd know what to say or how to act in the presence of these people.

She'd led a privileged and protected life as the daughter of William Van Patten. He'd made his money in banking and coal, but those were things Louisa never thought about. Lately, though, she'd become acutely aware of her pampered life, living in a 122-room mansion on Long Island's Gold Coast, taking shopping trips to Paris, and spending summers in Italy and Provence.

Each time she tried to talk to her father about her interest in helping others through social work, he'd laughed derisively and warned her not to start feeling guilty about money and position. He grumbled that this was exactly what he was afraid of when she'd enrolled at Bryn Mawr. A little education? Well, that was all right, he supposed, but an advanced degree was overkill, he said. He'd warned her not to turn into a bluestocking. She had laughed at the old-fashioned term and told him there was no reason to be afraid of a modern woman.

"Modern woman? Is that what you call those floozies traipsing around after that Sanger woman? I call that immoral."

"Being a follower of Margaret Sanger doesn't make anyone immoral, Father. Neither does advocating birth control."

His jaw hardened. "That is hardly an expression a lady of your breeding should be using."

"What? Oh, you mean birth control? Well, never mind." She made a dismissive gesture with a wave of her hand. "I'm not talking about that. I simply want you to understand that I want to help the underprivileged, Father. I'm thinking of going into the professional study of the minds of those poor unfortunate deviants who make up so much of the population of the underprivileged."

A red tide had come up over her father's face from his neck. "Are you talking about psychiatry?"

"Yes, I am. As I've told you before, I'm interested in eugenics as a means of stemming the tide of the deviant population—the epileptic, the feebleminded. I feel that if I can study the minds of—"

Her father's red face paled dramatically. "If you want to help the underprivileged, found a charity. Suitable pursuit for a woman of your class is definitely not psychiatry. I put my foot down there. I won't stand for you mingling with idiots and imbeciles." He turned away quickly and disappeared into another part of the house.

She'd already met Anne Harris by the time she had that conversation with her father. Anne was four years older than Louisa and held a certificate in nursing from Bellevue Hospital in New York when she came to Bryn Mawr to speak to women interested in social work and public health. Louisa's letter to her was answered by an invitation to meet for tea so they could discuss Louise accompanying her on a visit to her client in Charlottesville, Virginia. Anne was eager to grant Louisa's request, and they agreed to schedule the visit after the semester ended. Louisa told her father that her train trip to Virginia was to consult with Mrs. Harris about the possibility of starting a charity for indigent women. It annoyed her to have to placate him. After all, she was almost twenty-one. Until she reached that milestone, however, he would continue to control her purse strings.

Louisa's father had agreed, reluctantly, to allow her to make the trip after he was assured that Mrs. Harris was a respectable woman with a respectable position in Charlottesville. As Louisa had antici-pated, he asked for no details about the proposed charity.

It continued to be impossible to discuss improving the human race by means of birth control or by sterilization of imbeciles and morons, who, in her observation, included so many in the ranks of the poor. Even if he favored implementing the science of eugenics, or even understood it, he most certainly wouldn't discuss it with her. He would be shocked that Lemuel Ross, the young lawyer from Richmond and the man she loved, had been the first to initiate a discussion of the subject with her. Father was fond of Lemuel, and it would never do for him to know the things the young man talked about with his daughter.

She'd been waiting almost twenty minutes in Anne's outer of-fice where the secretary had instructed her to sit, her anxiety fer-menting into dread. When at last Anne walked in from the hallway, she appeared flustered.

"My dear Louisa," she said, going to her. Louisa stood, and Anne kissed her briefly on the cheek. "I'm so sorry to keep you waiting. The district supervisor called me to his office for a meeting quite unexpectedly. I did my best to get away, but...well, will you ever forgive me?"

"Of course," Louisa answered. "Please don't concern yourself. You must be terribly busy. Perhaps I should come back another—"

"Don't even think of postponing this." Anne dumped a pack-et of papers on her secretary's desk. "You've come all the way to Charlottesville on your break from school that you should be spend-ing with your parents. I've inconvenienced you by forcing you to wait, and I won't compound it by being so thoughtless as to send you back empty-handed, so to speak."

"Please don't consider it an inconvenience. I..."

"File those for me, please, Thelma," Anne said to her secretary. Then she called out to Louisa over her shoulder, "I'll just get my medical bag and my client notes, and we'll be on our way." She disappeared into her office briefly before she came out with a clip-board and a satchel.

Louisa had to hurry to keep up with Anne's brisk pace to her motor car parked outside the county courthouse. The motor car, which Louisa's father still referred to as a petrol wagon, was a Ford, several years old and a bit worse for the wear. Anne went to the front of the automobile and gave the engine a quick turn of the crank and then slid under the wheel, engaging the pedals and twisting the steering wheel in an expert manner. There was much for Louisa to admire in a woman whose independence had been forced upon her as Anne's must have been, while her own brand of independence was stolen and camouflaged with convention.

"We're going to see Emma Buck first," Anne said as she maneuvered the Ford from the parking lot. "Perplexing case. I've tried to put her in touch with at least half a dozen charities, but they only give her temporary help—food, occasionally clothing for her or her two children. I know at least one group has tried to help her find work, but she won't work. She won't provide for her children."

"Then how do they survive?"

Anne turned toward her and, raising her eyebrows, gave her a look that Louisa could only interpret as she'd asked a ridiculous question. "Well, when I say she doesn't work, that's not exactly true. She finds work on the streets, shall we say."

"Oh, I see." Louisa prayed that she wasn't blushing, that she didn't appear as naive as she feared.

"This is going to be an eye-opener for you; I'm certain of that," Anne said. "It wasn't so very long ago that I was in your position. By that, I mean I was full of theories about indigents and how to help them, but until you actually go among them, you have no concept of the reality of their plight."

"That's exactly why I so eagerly accepted your invitation to do this fieldwork, my dear Anne. I want to experience reality. I want to understand it." They had reached a particularly bumpy stretch of unpaved road, and Louisa found she had to grasp the armrest with one hand to keep her balance while she held on to her hat with the other hand so it wouldn't fly off her head.

Anne turned toward Louisa long enough to give her a brilliant smile. "I knew the moment I met you that you were particularly suited to this work." It was only a few minutes later that she slowed the car and maneuvered in front of a dilapidated structure that could hardly be called a house. "And here we are," she said, gathering up her clipboard and bag.

"It looks like...like a chicken coop." Louisa hadn't meant to sound so shocked.

"That's exactly what it is." The words came out with Anne's breath at the end of a deep sigh. "I have no idea who owns this rundown shack, but it did once house chickens, and when it was abandoned, Emma moved in." A small laugh escaped Anne's throat. "It still smells like chicken shit."

Louisa involuntarily cut her eyes toward Anne. She'd never heard her use crude language. She made no reply, thinking that working among the lower classes undoubtedly fostered such slips into vulgarity. Instead of criticizing her, she laughed as Anne had, and Anne gave her a knowing rise of her eyebrows.

Anne's knock at the door brought a hoarse voice from the inside telling them to come in. As they entered, a fleshy, ill-kempt woman was smoothing her dress. What appeared to be a plastered-on smile disappeared when she saw the two women.

"Oh, it's you, Harris," the woman said, making it obvious she'd expected someone else. She stared at Louisa.

"Miss Van Patten is here to assist me, Emma," Anne said.

Emma continued to stare. "Assist you? With what?"

"With my rounds," Anne answered.

Emma appeared neither satisfied nor dissatisfied with the vague answer. "Where you from?" she asked, still looking at Louisa.

"My home is in Long Island."

"Never heard of it."

"It's in the state of New York. Not far from the city." Anne spoke without looking up as she flipped over pages on her clipboard.

"New York? Shoulda guessed," Emma said.

"Miss Van Patten is doing work at Bryn Mawr College soon, and she's interested in—"

"College? Shoulda guessed that, too," Emma interrupted, scrutinizing Louisa even more carefully.

Louisa could feel her eyes taking in the yellow wool gabardine of her fashionably narrow skirt and matching loose-fitting jacket, as well as the perfectly matched hat she wore atop her pinned-up hair. She'd chosen her costume carefully, hoping not to appear ostentatious. She was now keenly aware that she hadn't succeeded.

"Emma, I told you to clean this place," Anne said, glancing around at the unmade bed, the stack of dishes crusted with dried food in a wash pan, and a dirty mop propped in a corner.

"Yeah, you did." There was no mistaking the defiance in Emma's voice.

"Why don't you do it?"

"Ain't got time."

"You have to take the time," Anne persisted. "It's not a fit place to bring up children. Where are the children anyway?"

Emma shrugged.

"They should be in school." Anne was growing frustrated.

"Yeah, well, I guess that's where they are." Emma reached for the makings to roll a cigarette and seemed distracted.

"You guess? Don't you know?" Anne's voice rose with her frustration. "Doris hasn't run away again, has she?"

"Not that I know of," Emma said, drawing smoke into her lungs.

Louisa looked on, both appalled and fascinated. The woman was being purposefully defiant. It was clear she didn't like Anne's interference.

"She ain't run away," Emma said as she plopped down to sit on the edge of the bed, leaving Anne and Louisa standing. "The school would let me know if she did. They always does."

"Is there enough food for you and the children?" Anne asked as she penciled something onto her clipboard papers. She raised her eyes to look around the ramshackle dwelling. "It doesn't appear there is, but I can recommend a charity you can contact for—"

"Don't need no charity," Emma said, straightening herself and pulling her shoulders back as she sat on the bed. "I got money. I can feed my kids."

Anne shook her head. "If your money is coming from prostitution again, you know the county can't allow—"

"Ain't none of your damn business where my money comes from," Emma blurted. "But if you must know, I got a inheritance."

"An inheritance?" Anne glanced at Louisa as if to confirm her disbelief.

"It's in the bank. My father left it to me."

"Which bank?" Anne asked.

Emma turned away and refused to answer at first. "Don't know which bank," she finally said in a voice that was almost a whisper. It was followed by another silence during which she kept her head turned away from the two women.

"Excuse me, ma'am," Louisa said. "Perhaps I can help. My father is a banker, and he may be able to help you locate the funds."

Emma turned toward Louisa, her eyes wide with a kind of hope that Louisa found almost unbearable to witness. "If I could get that money..."

"He'd need to know your father's name, where he lived, and when he deposited it. Maybe how much it is."

The hope in her eyes faded, replaced by a wary expression. "Need to know my business, would he?"

Louisa recoiled slightly. "Only if you wish to tell him."

Emma's hard mouth softened briefly. She brought what was now a stub of the cigarette to her mouth and inhaled. "I'll think about it," she said through the smoke in her mouth. Then she coughed, a wet, rattling sound.

The sound got Anne's attention. "That cough. It's come back," she said, pulling a stethoscope from her bag. "I'll have a listen. We don't want the pneumonia to return."

"Ain't pneumonia. Got strangled on the smoke, that's all," Emma said, but she unbuttoned the top of her threadbare dress and waited for the stethoscope.

Anne listened for a while and nodded her head. "Doesn't sound like pneumonia. Not yet at least." She picked up one of Emma's hands and looked at her palms.

Louisa could see that they were mottled and scarred, obvious signs of a previous outbreak of syphilis. She knew that from her textbooks, although she'd never actually seen a person with syphilis.

Anne put her stethoscope in her bag before she spoke again. "I want you to listen to me now, Emma. I'm going to say this as plain and as carefully as I can. Are you listening?" She spoke as if she was speaking to a child, and Emma looked at her with the same defiance a wayward child might have. "You are obviously not well. You don't have any food in the house, you aren't sure where your children are, and you most certainly are plying your trade on the streets, so I am recommending—"

"What's that mean, plikin' a trade on the streets?"

"It means you're a prostitute, Emma."

"Fuck you."

Louisa couldn't stop herself from drawing in a sharp breath.

Anne appeared undaunted. "I'm afraid I'm going to have to recommend that the county take your children and place them in—"

Emma shot up from the edge of the bed and flared at Anne, taking a step toward her. "Get out, bitch! Nobody ain't takin' my kids. Get out."

Anne took a step backward, and Louisa moved toward her, thinking for one foolish moment that she would protect her.

"Get out! Both you bitches. Get out!" She shoved at Anne and then at Louisa, forcing them toward the door.

"I'm sorry, ma'am," Louisa said. "We really didn't mean to—"

"Louisa!" Anne's tone was sharp and urgent. "Come with me." She grabbed Louisa's arm and pulled her out the door and to the car where she all but pushed her into the passenger seat while she once again turned the crank to start the engine.

Louisa felt her heart hammering at her chest. "Good Lord!" she said as Anne got into the car.

"Don't let it upset you," Anne said.

"Well, I can certainly see why *she* was upset. The idea of taking her children away—"

"Of course it upset her," Anne said, cutting in before Louisa could finish. "But surely you can see that the children would be better off."

"I have no doubt of that, but"—she paused a moment—"she's an uneducated woman. That must make it hard for her to understand that you're trying to help."

"She's more than uneducated, Louisa. The woman is mentally defective. Surely you can see that."

"I'm not certain—"

"Well, she is," Anne said, cutting in again. "I would say her mentality is that of a twelve-year-old."

"Oh!" Louisa was a little taken aback by the assessment. "You are undoubtedly right. You have ever so much more experience than I do." Her brow wrinkled as her interest grew. "And her children? Are they mentally defective as well?"

"I don't know about that," Anne replied. "The oldest child is in a foster home and seems all right. The boy—I think his name is Roy—doesn't do well in school, but I don't know if that's because he's mentally defective. You know how boys are. And then there's Doris. The only thing I know about her is that she ran away from a foster home and is such a mess nobody can handle her. You know what I mean? She won't stay in school. That sort of thing."

"Maybe because her mother hasn't taught her any better?"

"Could be. I don't know, but I do know she'd be better off if she was placed in the county orphanage."

"Well..." Louisa said, mulling it over in her mind.

"What?"

"I was just thinking. Have you ever heard of the science of eugenics, Anne?"

"Eugenics? I'm not sure. Is it something I should know?"

"It's the science of improving the human race through hereditary qualities."

Anne laughed. "How can you change heredity?"

"You can't. But you can control it. The idea, you see, is to sterilize carriers of defective qualities...like mental deficiency."

"Sterilize?"

"Don't be shocked, Anne. Think about it. Most of the crimes committed in all human societies are committed by people who are mentally and morally defective. So the solution is to surgically sterilize those who are carriers of such defects."

"Surgically? Are you speaking of castration?" There was no escaping the astonishment in Anne's voice.

"In some cases. Oh, I know it sounds drastic, but men can be sterilized by other means. It's possible to sever the vas tubes. You know, the tubes that carry the sperm. It's rarely a fatal operation, and for women, it's almost as simple. It's a matter of removing the fallopian tubes."

"A salpingectomy."

"Exactly! So you have heard of it."

"I'm a trained nurse, remember." Anne sounded defensive.

"Of course you are. Then you must understand how this policy could be beneficial. It doesn't interfere with a person's daily life. He or she can be released to lead lives that are productive to the extent of their capabilities, but without creating a society of lunatics and morons and epileptics."

"Interesting," Anne said.

"Oh, I know you're skeptical. I was, too, at first. But it's all the talk in New York now, especially among all the best people. Mr. Alexander Bell, Mr. Thomas Edison. You've heard of them, I know. They've come out publically in favor of implementing the science."

Anne parked the car in front of the courthouse where her office was located. She switched off the engine and turned to Louisa. "I can see the merits, of course. It's just that sterilization seems so, well, permanent."

Louisa felt a rush of excitement at being able to discuss such heady matters with her mentor. "Of course it's permanent," she said. "Isn't that the idea?"

"Maybe, but shouldn't a person have some, well, control over her own body?"

"Some of us, of course. But for epileptics and morons who are incapable of knowing what's best, no."

Anne frowned as she opened the door to get out of the car. Louisa got out as well and hurried to catch up with her. "I know what you're thinking," Louisa continued, "but Lemuel says the family could designate a guardian and, of course, hire a lawyer to make certain the person's rights are protected. Or the state could appoint both if the person is indigent."

"Lemuel?"

"Lemuel Ross. Remember him?"

"Ross? The young lawyer from that prominent Richmond family? The one who came to talk to your senior class about public policy?"

Louisa smiled and nodded.

Anne gave her a knowing look. "I take it you've gotten to know him."

"You could say that." Louisa was still smiling, and she felt herself blushing.

"Well, well, you must tell me all about it, but first. . ." She stopped speaking and looked at something in the distance. Louisa followed her gaze across the street and a few blocks away. "There's Emma in front of the grocery store," Anne said. "She must be looking for customers."

"Oh!" Louisa took a breath and said no more. She didn't want to appear shocked. She wanted desperately to be able to display her maturity and sophistication to Anne.

"I hope her anger has cooled by now," Anne said. "I'd like to talk to her again. I really need to persuade her to give those children up to the orphanage."

"Perhaps I can help," Louisa said. She was already walking toward Emma, hoping Anne saw her as confident rather than brash.

10

CARRIE

Mrs. Dobbs had sent me to town to buy baking powder from the grocery store next door to Woolworth's, and that's when I saw Mama. Doris and Roy were nowhere in sight, but there were two women sitting on the bench with her. One of them had a long face and lips that looked like she didn't approve of something. She was dressed in white like a nurse. Her hair was partly hidden by a white cap. The other was prettier. She'd removed her hat, and ginger-colored curls tumbled to her shoulders. She wore a dress the color of morning sunshine that I could tell, even from a distance, was made of something soft and expensive.

I hung back, hoping none of them would see me. They seemed to be discussing something important—so important that the nurse kept hitting her small, bony right fist in the palm of her left hand while Mama shook her head like she was disagreeing with her. Once she let out a cry of "No!" that sounded as if she could be in pain. With that, the pretty woman reached a gloved hand across the nurse's lap and touched Mama's arm. The woman said something so low and soft I couldn't hear it.

They talked, or argued, for several more minutes while I watched, hiding in the shadows of the grocery doorway. Mama stood up quick like she was mad and walked away. She was wailing, "No! No, I won't let you do such a thing. I got my rights!"

Both women called after her. They didn't try to follow her

though. Instead they looked around like they was uneasy, like they was afraid they would attract attention. The nurse shook her head and said something to the pretty woman just before they turned away from Mama and started walking away.

I ducked inside the store quick as I could and hurried to the back before I even turned around to look for them. When I was sure the two women hadn't entered the store, I started to look for the Clabber Girl Baking Powder that Mrs. Dobbs wanted. It didn't take me long to find it where it always was, on the bottom shelf of the second aisle. By the time I paid for it and stepped outside, the nurse and the other woman were nowhere in sight, but Mama was back on the bench in front of Woolworth's smoking a cigarette and staring at nothing.

With the can of baking powder under my arm, I walked toward her kind of slow and stopped a few feet away.

"Hello, Mama." I know I sounded choked as I spoke because the word had a funny taste on my tongue. Mama turned toward the sound of my voice. "Oh, it's you." The words came out with a lazy river of smoke. "Whadda you want?"

"I just wanted to see if you was...to see how you was doing."

Mama looked away and took another drag from the cigarette. "Doin' all right."

It seemed like neither of us said anything for a really long time. I just stood there staring at the cigarette. I'd seen women smoke before, but it still looked odd to me. The thing she held between her thumb and forefinger wasn't one of the new ready-rolls some of the well-to-do men smoked. It was the kind people rolled theirselves—ragged and misshapen. Like Mama.

I finally managed to say, "Good. That's good. That you're feeling okay, I mean." I started to feel embarrassed after another long silence followed, and I turned to walk away.

"No, it ain't good," Mama said to my back. I turned around to look at her, and she spoke again. "Damned county nurse wants to take my babies away from me."

"Take your babies?"

"Roy and Doris. They say I ain't fit to take care of 'em. But they ain't gettin' 'em."

"Oh" was all I could think to say. I was thinking how I'd always been told that she gave me away when I was only three. I'd never heard that it bothered her. Were Roy and Doris more valuable?

"That pinched-up Nurse Harris and that other one, the pretty one. Said her name was Van Patten or something like that. High-tone slut if you ask me. Don't know shit. Neither one of 'em. They don't know shit about me or my kids. Want me to give 'em up. I already had to give up one, thanks to that damn Shackelford."

I had no idea who "that damn Shackelford" might be, but my mind and my heart were clinging to the other words Mama had said. It sounded as if maybe there was just a little regret that she'd had to give me away.

"You're doin' good though, ain't ye?" Mama threw her cigarette to the sidewalk and stepped on it with the toe of her worn, scuffed shoes. They were the old-fashioned kind that laced up like boots, the style nobody wore anymore. The cigarette lay splayed and tattered on the sidewalk.

"I'm doin' just fine," I said. I wished I could tell her the truth— that I wasn't just fine because I wasn't allowed to go to school anymore, but it wouldn't do anybody any good for me to say it.

"The Dobbses is good to you, ain't they?"

"I guess so."

"Whadda you mean you guess so? You ain't hungry, are you? You get three meals a day. They don't beat you, 'cept when you need it, I bet. You ought to be grateful for their kindness."

"Yes ma'am."

Mama laughed. "You got manners. More than I can say for Doris. She's a pistol, that girl is." She sprawled herself on the bench, each arm draped over the back, her legs stretched in front of her while she stared ahead at the same nothing she was looking at earlier.

Once again I couldn't think of anything more to say. I kept my eyes on Mama a few seconds longer and then looked down at my shoes. I got them new a year ago. They were still in fairly good shape, even if they were beginning to pinch a little. I guess I ought to be grateful to have 'em.

Mama looked at me. "Well, go on then."

I turned without looking at her and hurried away. I was almost a block away when I finally looked back. Someone had come up to talk to Mama. A man. Mama stood up and walked away with him. The way she walked, heavy and lumbering, made me think she must be tired.

"What taken you so long?" Mrs. Dobbs asked when I let myself in the back door, carrying the baking powder.

"It didn't take me very long," I said.

"Well, a normal person coulda done it in half the time. It ain't but a few blocks to the store."

"No they couldn't. Not in *half* the time."

"Don't you talk back to me, Carrie Buck!" Mrs. Dobbs said, turning away from the pot she was stirring and shaking the spoon at me.

I ducked my head and kept my voice low. "I'm sorry, ma'am."

"I suppose you was lollygaggin' around with boys instead of comin' straight home."

"No, ma'am, I wasn't."

"Yeah, like you wasn't runnin' off to the woods with that Hopkins boy."

"I never run off to no woods with nobody. We just went fishin' and—"

"I-said-don't-talk-back-to-meeee," Mrs. Dobbs said in that sing-songy voice again, this time without bothering to turn around.

"Yes ma'am."

"I swear I have to watch you ever' minute to make sure you get anything done," Mrs. Dobbs said, more to herself than to me. "Now wash your hands and make them biscuits. Mr. Dobbs is expecting 'em for supper," she added, raising her voice.

I wanted to tell her it wasn't true that I had to be watched every minute. I wanted to say I was much better at doing her work without being told than Lucy had been when she still lived with them. But I kept silent and made the biscuits.

They turned out light and fluffy the way they always did when there was baking powder to add to the dough. Mr. Dobbs ate almost a whole pan. I remember one time when Waverly winked at me from across the table and told his mother he wished I'd make biscuits like that every night.

"I'd marry you when you growed up if you did," he'd said. That had made Lucy spew milk out of her mouth and punch Waverly on the arm while she laughed at him. Mrs. Dobbs laughed, too, and told him he was a caution to talk like that. Mr. Dobbs hadn't said anything. He'd just buttered another biscuit.

Later, when the dishes were washed and put away, I lingered by the open back door to enjoy the cool breeze of early evening. I heard Mr. Dobbs speaking to his wife as they sat in their rocking chairs under the willow tree.

"Had to threaten to take ol' Emma in again. I swear, sometimes I think she wants to get caught whorin' around just so's I'll take her in and give her a place to sleep."

"Leaves them kids to fend for theirselves, I guess," Mrs. Dobbs said. "County ought to take 'em away from her."

Mr. Dobbs's answer was a loud burp.

I went to my room and held Annabelle close since there was no one in the room to tell me I was too big to do that. I didn't whisper to her anymore, but I spoke to her with my mind and told her that someday I would have a real Annabelle, a real baby girl, and I would never give her away to anyone, no matter what. I would love her and keep her always.

From: Anne Harris, District Nurse, Charlottesville, Albemarle County, Virginia
To: Mr. J. T. Dobbs, Peace Officer, Charlottesville, Virginia
October 1919

Dear Mr. Dobbs,

Your inquiry to Judge Charles Shackleford regarding the possibility of any form of disposition for Emma Buck has been forwarded to me with instructions to inform you of the particulars in the matter.

I must apologize to you for the long delay in responding, but since you are also a public servant, you will understand the enormous weight of work that is placed upon us who serve the citizens of the county and city, as well as the fact that there are not enough hours in the day to get all that is necessary done in a timely manner.

In response to your inquiry, I will say that I have known Emma Buck for several years and have from time to time taken it upon myself to contact various charity organizations to give her relief from her poverty. I am afraid the efforts of these groups can provide only temporary relief since Mrs. Buck seems either incapable or unwilling to work and take care of herself or of her children. Her two younger children have been sent to foster homes at times but with limited success, at least for the daughter, Doris. She has run away three times. However, we will continue our endeavors to see that she is suitably placed.

We who are servants of the county are, of course, eternally grateful to you and Mrs. Dobbs for your excellent care of the oldest Buck offspring. We have had no report of any problem with her except for a minor incident relayed to us a few years ago by Miss Watson of McGuffy School regarding the girl writing inappropriate notes to boys in class, which you and Mrs. Dobbs handled with efficiency.

As for your mention of Emma Buck's drunkenness, I am unaware of any persistent problem on her part. However, if, as you suggested, there is such a problem, it is not within the realm of my own or the Health Department's responsibility to recommend disposition. That falls within the right and duty of peace officers like you to see that she is incarcerated if the problem persists. I am, of course, aware of certain innuendoes concerning her shameful profession, which I am sure you agree constitutes a blight upon the society of the majority of us who are diligent in our pursuit of morality. However, that, too, must be dealt with by your own department.

If I can be of further service, do not hesitate to contact me.

Yours very truly,
Anne Harris, RN

11

CARRIE

I tried to sneak out and see my mama as much as I could because I felt so blue. I was still sad about school and about Waverly marrying Florence, who wasn't even very pretty.

A lot of the time it was hard to find Mama, and even when I did see her, it didn't help me feel much better. She always looked so worn out and dirty. Doris and Roy always looked dirty, too. Whenever I could, I gave them money or bought them something. I always hoped they spent the money on food, or maybe soap.

Somehow the Dobbses found out about me seeing Mama and the kids. I learned that when I overheard them talking one day. I also found out something else that I didn't completely understand.

The two of them were in the living room, and I was in kitchen. You would think that after living in that house as long as they had, they would realize how easy it was to listen in from the kitchen to talk in the living room.

"Well, it's natural that a girl would want to see after her own mama," Mrs. Dobbs said.

Mr. Dobbs gave her a look like he was disgusted. "I heard you tell me a hundred times you didn't like Carrie being around that woman. Then I start trying to get her off the streets of Charlottesville, and you tell me I oughtn't to do that."

"I ain't saying you oughtn't to do anything. I just said how Carrie feels is natural."

"You're taking up for her, that's what. On account of you think she's your little pet. Next thing, you're going to be telling me you never said she sasses you sometimes."

"Sure she does, but that's natural, too. Kind of."

"What do you mean, 'kind of'?" By now, I think Mr. Dobbs was beginning to lose interest in what he seemed to think was Mrs. Dobbs not making any sense, and he was looking around for the paper to read.

"Well, what I mean is, it's just a stage she's going through," Mrs. Dobbs said. "Lucy used to get sassy with me sometimes. They grow out of it."

Mr. Dobbs gave a satisfied grumble when he located the newspaper and settled down into an easy chair.

"When is it going to happen?" Mrs. Dobbs waited several seconds for an answer until she decided he was ignoring her. "J. T.?"

The sound of his name got his attention. "What?" he asked without taking his eyes from the paper.

"I said when is it going to happen?"

"When is what going to happen?"

Mr. Dobbs didn't even hear Mrs. Dobbs's disgusted huff, and I don't think he even knew that she'd left the room. He thought she was still listening when he finally spoke. "I already signed the papers. Probably have to take her to the courthouse before the end of the week."

12

EMMA

"**W**hat do the bastards know? Nothing about how things really are out there in the world, that's for sure." Emma didn't speak the words aloud. She just let the unspoken sound of them tickle her mind while she stared at the ornate metal tiles of the courtroom ceiling, pretending she didn't know what was happening.

Truth was she really didn't know *everything* that was happening. She didn't know what they meant by *interrogatories* or *deposition*. She sure didn't know what *eugenics* meant. Probably some kind of disease. Like syphilis maybe. What she was certain of, however, was that she had to play her role just right. Act like she was a little off. Not crazy—that could get her in big trouble. Just not quite right.

It was Jake Collins who told her not to try to fight the bastards but to go along with them and make them think she was a little off. Jake was one of her customers. He worked for the city, and he knew about stuff like that. He said life in the Colony was good—roof over your head, three meals a day, nothing to worry about. Said he knew because they put his sister in there since she had epileptic fits. Said the state would take care of the kids, too, if they put her in the Colony. He had convinced her to give in and let the county put her in the place. Now all she had to do was make it happen.

It felt like an icebox in the courtroom, even though it was

already April. Warm enough for the trees to bud. Emma pulled her thin sweater tighter around her fleshy arms. Funny how she could feel so cold and still sweat where her thick, fleshy thighs pressed together as she sat on the uncomfortable courtroom chair.

Judge Charlie Shackelford was up there in his black robe seated behind that high desk. He had just told her to be seated. Now he was going on about something else, talking to those doctors who would decide whether or not she was feebleminded. One of the doctors said his name was Flippen. Emma wondered if he might be kin to the Flippens who lived over in the Blue Ridge. Probably not. They were mountain folk. Not like this doctor with his slicked-down hair and his high-priced suit. There was another doctor sitting at the table with him. They both looked well-fed and serious-minded. Fat and sassy was what she'd call them.

Charlie Shackelford cleared his throat. "I said state your name, please."

"Emma Buck." He knew what her name was because she'd stood in front of him so many times, accused of vagrancy and prostitution. She didn't see why he had to ask this time. Seems like he was the one who was feebleminded.

She told herself to pay closer attention. She didn't want to mess up this hearing. She was pretty sure that if she got sent to the Colony, there would be no more filthy drunks rutting her for two bits, no more teeth knocked out just for the hell of it.

She already knew she could rest easy about her oldest child, Carrie. She had to be, what, thirteen, maybe fourteen years old now? The state took her away when she was three and gave her to J. T. Dobbs and his wife. Said Emma wasn't good enough to take care of her. Said the kid ought not to be around all them drunks that paid her to fuck them. Well, they were right about that. Carrie was better off even if Emma couldn't stand the sight of the Dobbses' snooty faces.

Do-gooders. Thought they were better than everybody else.

As for the other two kids, she'd been assured by that Nurse

Harris that they'd be placed in foster homes. She now knew that was the best she could do for them. Still, it was hard to admit you couldn't take care of your kids and had to give them up. Roy would be all right. He had a head on his shoulders just like Carrie. Doris would be, too, but somebody would have to tame her first.

Dr. Flippen had just asked her another question, and she forced herself to pay attention to the matters at hand and stop thinking about the kids.

"I repeat, Miz Buck, when were you born?"

"November of eighteen and seventy-two."

"What day in November?"

Emma shrugged.

"You mean you don't know the day on which you were born?" The doctor sounded impatient.

Emma shrugged again. How was she supposed to know the day? Nobody had ever told her.

"Can you at least tell me *where* you were born?"

The tone of his voice angered Emma. Smart-ass. Thought he was better than she was. But she did her best to push the anger aside. After all, she was trying to appear feebleminded. She reminded herself again that she didn't want to overdo it, didn't want to look all the way crazy and end up in the insane asylum. She decided to answer honestly.

"Albemarle."

The doctor seemed to accept that she meant Albemarle County, and there was no town to name since she was born at home out in the country. Just before the next question, she noticed a smart-ass smile flicker across his face.

"Are you married, Miz Buck?"

"I'm a widow," she said, and wished she could add *you son of a bitch.* Frank Buck had been her lawful husband, and nobody could say he wasn't. Somewhere she had the marriage license to prove it. He died in a car wreck right after Carrie was born and left her with nothing but the clothes on her back. She had to find a way to make a living the best way she could.

Next the doctor asked her if she had children, and she was so mad she dared not speak, so she held up three fingers.

"Are any of them mentally defective?" he asked.

"No, of course not." Her response was barely audible as she tried to hold back her wrath. What did her kids have to do with this anyway?

Next he had her name the colors of some strips of paper he had, and then he had her do stupid things like stand up, raise both of her hands, and close her eyes. She knew she did all of them right, but she tried to be slow about it so it would look like she wasn't too sharp. She began to worry that maybe she should have deliberately misnamed some of the colors or just raised one hand when he told her to raise both. When he asked her next to pick up a book and hand it to the judge, she pretended she didn't understand and prayed she wasn't overdoing it.

"I'm going to have to report you incapable of carrying out a simple errand." Dr. Flippen had a frown of self-importance on his brow as he spoke.

Emma smiled secretly to herself.

"Have you ever been convicted of a crime?" the doctor asked.

"Yeah, prostitution." She'd heard that if you admitted you were a prostitute, it would count toward feeblemindedness. Didn't make sense, but what the hell, a lot of things didn't make sense sometimes. But she *had* been locked up for prostitution—more than once. That much was true.

"Moral delinquency," he said, writing it down. When he looked up from his notes, he asked, "Do you have illegitimate children?"

"Yeah, the last two," she said and pretended to yawn.

"You're saying you haven't conducted yourself in a proper conjugal manner," he said.

She frowned. What the hell did that mean? Was he trying to trick her somehow? "I'm saying I got two bastards," she said. She saw the doctor glance at the other doctor sitting at the table and taking notes. She saw the way they raised their eyebrows and tried to suppress their grins.

"To what degree have you carried out a legitimate commercial function?"

Emma frowned again. The son of a bitch *was* trying to trick her. She didn't know what to say, so she remained silent and stared at the doctor with contempt in her eyes.

"Has never supported herself," the doctor said, mouthing the words he wrote down when her answer wasn't forthcoming. "It seems to me you could do housework, under supervision, of course."

"I got income," Emma said, thinking she wasn't going to let him get by with insulting her and making her feel like scum. "From my father's estate. He was a man of property." Then she wished she hadn't said it. It was none of his goddamned business and had nothing to do with placing her in the Colony. But it was true. Her father had left her some money—something like $400, maybe. Her uncle Sam Dudley said it was supposed to be in one of the banks there in Charlottesville. It was just that she had no idea which one or how to go about getting it out. That woman Nurse Harris had brought with her had offered to help, but Emma was suspicious of her.

Dr. Flippen put down his pen. "All right, Emma, it's time to ascertain your physical condition." He stood, picked up a medical bag, and walked around to her side of the table. Emma noticed that he'd stopped referring to her as Mrs. Buck. "Have you ever had any serious illness?" he asked as he placed a stethoscope on her chest. She could feel the cold steel through the thin cotton material of her faded dress.

"Rheumatism," she said. "And I took pneumonia twice." He had her open her mouth, and she saw how he turned his face away from her and wrinkled his nose like he didn't like the smell of her breath.

"Have you ever had syphilis?" He sounded as if he was trying not to breathe the fetid air.

Emma's response was a noncommittal grunt.

Dr. Flippen glanced at the other doctor. "I believe the notes in her medical history will confirm that she has suffered from this affliction in the past."

The doctor nodded and shuffled though pages of notes he had in front of him.

"Do you still have syphilis?" Dr. Flippen asked.

"You're the doctor; you tell me." She made no attempt to hide her disdain this time.

Within a few minutes she was told the hearing was over and that she was free to leave. She slept, shivering on a park bench that night, since the shack she'd called home had been condemned as unsafe.

Order of Commitment

April 15, 1920

To the Sheriff, or Sergeant, of the City of Charlottesville and to Dr. A. S. Priddy, MD, Superintendent of the Virginia State Colony for Epileptics and Feebleminded of Madison Heights (Virginia), greetings:

Whereas, I, C. D. Shackelford, a judge of Charlottesville, and J. G. Flippen and W. H. Turner Jr., two physicians constituting a commission of inquiry, etc. into the mental condition of the said Emma Buck, have this day adjudged the said Emma Buck to be feebleminded. I, C. D. Shackelford, do in the name of the Commonwealth, command you, the said sheriff or sergeant, to make provisions for the suitable and proper care and custody of the said feebleminded person, and you, the said Superintendent of the Colony for Epileptics and Feebleminded, are hereby required to receive into the said Colony the said Emma Buck to be treated and cared for as a feebleminded person.

13

CARRIE

"**M**y mama went where? Madison Heights? Where's that?"

"South of here. Outside of Lynchburg." Mr. Dobbs seemed a little edgy as he answered me. If I didn't know better, I would think he was acting like he'd just done something he shouldn't have. I didn't know what that might be though. After all, he was a policeman.

"How come she went there?" I was standing in front of him as he sat in his easy chair. For once, though, he wasn't reading the paper.

Mr. Dobbs started to say something. "On account of she's feeb—"

"It's a place where she'll get took care of," Mrs. Dobbs said, butting in even though she knew Mr. Dobbs hated it when she did that. This time, though, he didn't seem to mind. He even looked like he was glad she'd done it and glad she'd come all the way into the living room instead of staying there in the doorway to the kitchen.

"Took care of?" I asked. "Is it a hospital? She ain't sick, is she?"

Mrs. Dobbs shook her head. "Oh no, nothin' like that. It's just a place for people who can't take care of theirselves."

"You mean my mama can't take care of herself?"

"Well, you know she never has been very good at that," Mrs. Dobbs said.

I knew she was right about my mama not ever being very good at taking care of herself. All I could bring myself to say was "I guess everybody thinks it's a good thing she got put away."

"Oh yes!" Mrs. Dobbs said. She looked relieved.

"But what about Doris and Roy?"

Mrs. Dobbs said, "Who?" Like she couldn't remember any Doris and Roy, but Mr. Dobbs jumped in and said they were both in the orphanage.

I didn't want to think about them being in an orphanage. I'd heard stories. As soon as Mrs. Dobbs saw the look on my face, she started trying to convince me they wouldn't be there very long. They would soon be adopted by families just like I was, she said. She kept saying, "Ain't that right, J. T.?"

"Oh, yeah," Mr. Dobbs said. "At least the boy might get adopted. I hear that girl keeps running away."

I saw right off that Mrs. Dobbs didn't like him saying that in front of me. She glared at him so hard she could have burned a hole right through him with her eyes. He didn't seem to notice. I saw then that Mrs. Dobbs was getting madder by the minute because of Mr. Dobbs being so thickheaded, but she just smiled in a false kind of way and told me there was nothing to worry about and that I'd better get the dishes done so I could go to bed since I had to get up early to help spade the garden for planting.

If there had been any way I could have got all the way out to Madison Heights, I would have gone to see Mama, but there was no way to do it. One time I even asked Mr. and Mrs. Dobbs to drive me out there, but Mrs. Dobbs said that was no place for a girl.

"Then how come it's all right for Mama?" I asked.

All she said was "Don't get sassy with me, young lady." And then she walked away.

I didn't have any better luck finding out where Doris and Roy were either. Mr. Dobbs said they were in an orphanage, but when I asked where the orphanage was, he claimed he didn't know. He knew. I know he did. He just didn't want me to know. It seemed like they thought my kin was poison or something. Of course, he reminded me that I would be in an orphanage, too, if it wasn't for the kindness of his heart.

Reminding me about the kindness of his heart didn't keep me from being mad at both of them. Every once in a while Mrs. Dobbs would complain that I was acting sullen, but I didn't care. I just went on being mad at them up until the day the telegram came.

It came with the news that Waverly fell off of something they called scaffolding while he was working on a ship. It came with the news that Waverly was dead.

His body came home on the train. Florence was on the same train. I had made up my mind not to like her, but I couldn't help feeling sorry for her. I felt sorry for all of us. It was just about the saddest thing any of us had been through, I guess.

It's hard for me to remember anything about the funeral, even though I was there. I know it was held in the church where we always went, but that's about all. It was like my body was there, but I wasn't. I felt that way for a long time afterward. I just went through the motions of doing my work, and I guess the Dobbses were doing the same thing.

All I know is that it felt like something had flown out of me on big black wings. It sort of felt like that thing was my dreams.

14

CARRIE

Mama had been in the Colony two years, and I'd never seen her. That's what they called it—the Colony. The full name was the Virginia State Colony for Epileptics and Feebleminded.

"My mama ain't feebleminded," I said to Mrs. Dobbs when I heard that word.

"You keep saying that over and over. Will you just hush? You don't know what you're talking about," Mrs. Dobbs said. She was working at the sewing machine at the time, her feet pumping up and down on the big pedal at the bottom to make the needle gouge its way into the soft blue cloth that was going to be a tiny shirt for Lucy's little boy.

"Well, she's not!" I said. "She's not feebleminded at all. Just because she never got to go to school much, don't—"

"I said hush," Mrs. Dobbs said, still pedaling and making the machine go rackety-rackety-rackety. "She's better off."

That made me feel bad, and I guess I was still feeling bad a few days later when Clarence stopped by to leave a saw Mr. Dobbs asked to borrow. He came in the Ford car his daddy bought. It made a funny coughing sound, but it got around really good.

"Well, don't you look down in the dumps," he said when he saw me. "What's the matter? You still mournin' ol' Waverly after all this time he's been gone?" He had put the saw in the shed just as I was coming in from the garden. Now he was standing next to the Ford, rubbing the fender like he was petting a cat.

"It's not Waverly. I know he's been gone a long time."

"Then what is it?" Clarence asked.

My first thought was not to answer him and just walk away, but when I looked at him, he didn't have that smart-alecky look on his face he usually had. Instead he was frowning just a little like he might really be concerned.

"It's my mama." I turned away quick, in case he was going to laugh and make fun of me and my mama.

"Oh yeah," he said. "I know about her bein' put in the insane asylum."

"It's not an insane asylum. It's the Colony."

Clarence snickered, but then after a few seconds, he said, "Shit, I guess that would kind of make you feel bad."

He'd surprised me again, but I still wouldn't look at him. I just shrugged my shoulders. "Mrs. Dobbs says she's better off."

"Sounds like you don't believe her." There was just a hint of a sneer in his voice. I couldn't tell if the sneer was aimed at me or Mrs. Dobbs.

I turned around to face him, feeling my anger come up. "How would I know? They won't let me see her."

"How come?" His face was blank.

"Too far."

"Where the hell is she?"

"Madison Heights. That's close to Lynchburg," I said.

He laughed, and I felt my body stiffen. "Lynchburg? I thought you was going to say Richmond or something. Lynchburg ain't far. But I didn't know that was where that asylum is."

I didn't answer, didn't try to tell him again that it wasn't an asylum, and I didn't look at him.

"Well, hell, if it'll cheer you up, I'll take you to see her."

I couldn't help but turn around again and stare at him. I couldn't believe what I'd just heard.

"Mama told me they put her away," Clarence said. "Does she have epileptic fits or something?"

"No." I was really uncomfortable with this conversation.

"Well, see if Aunt Alice will let you go. I'll drive you down to see her. Ain't but sixty-five miles. We can do that in two hours."

"All the way to Lynchburg in two hours?" I could hardly believe it.

"Yep." He gave the Ford a firm pat and an admiring glance. I could see that it was the drive he was interested in more than helping me. If he gave all of his attention to the automobile, maybe he wouldn't bother me.

"I hope it won't be dangerous to go that fast," I said.

As soon as I said that, I realized that it would probably give him an excuse to laugh at me, but he didn't seem to hear me. He was already turning the crank on the front of the Ford. The machine gave out a reluctant cough and a sputter and then another cough before it started it's rackety-rackety, and Clarence hurried to jump in the car. "I'll pick you up Sunday," he said as he drove away.

I dreaded asking Mrs. Dobbs to let me make the trip to see Mama. I knew she would have a fit and tell me I couldn't go. That she needed me at home to work. That it wasn't right for me to go off somewhere with a boy.

When I finally got the courage a few days later to ask her, she just looked at me for a few seconds like she was thinking it over. "Well, I guess it's natural you wantin' to see her," she said.

"Yes ma'am."

"Clarence says he'll take you?"

"Yes ma'am."

"You told me you hated that boy."

"Well, I do--did. But I think he's grown up a little."

"Wants to take you in that Ford his daddy bought, does he?"

I nodded.

She squinted at me for a few seconds, and I was thinking she was going to say I could go. Instead she said, "You got no business going off somewhere with a boy. What are you thinking?"

I ducked my head the way I always did when she scolded me. "I was just thinking that I wanted to see my mama."

"You're better off if you don't." That's all she said

I left the house and went outside to the garden. I tried not to think about Mama or Waverly or school or anything. I tried to think about all the weeds that needed pulling and the sparkly way they smelled when they came out of the earth. The way the dirt smelled like rich, thick secrets. The way the hot sun felt like melting butter running along my shoulder blades.

Thinking like that made me feel once again like I had left my body and was floating around somewhere else. I can't say where. Heaven maybe, except there were no streets of gold, no angels, and no God. Just blue light. I kind of liked the way it made me feel.

I was so numbed by that feeling that I didn't even notice when Clarence came rattling up in the Ford again. He was standing in front of me with his hands on his hips while I knelt next to a row of turnips. Finally, he spoke to me.

"Well?" He sounded like the old Clarence, impatient and demanding.

"Oh!" I struggled to my feet. "I didn't know you was here."

"Why not? You deaf or something?"

"No."

"Then you must be a moron."

"I'm not a moron." He was making me angry. Just like the old Clarence. I turned away from him because I didn't want him to see the tears that were spilling out of my eyes. I don't know why I was crying, except that it just seemed like everything was going wrong in my life. I hated being a poor-me whiner, though, and I didn't want him to know that was exactly what I was at that moment.

He reached out and grabbed my shoulder and turned me around to face him. "Ah, what are you crying about?" he asked.

"Nothing."

"You going with me Sunday or not?"

I shook my head.

"Why you"—he paused—"Oh, I get it. Aunt Alice and Uncle J. T. won't let you go."

"No, they won't," I said, wishing he would leave. I turned away from him and bent over to pick up the little garden pick I'd been using to uproot weeds. When I straightened, I sensed that he had been staring at me the whole time. I started to walk back to the house, but he reached for me again, stopping me.

"I'm, well, I'm sorry you're feeling so bad." After a few seconds he added, "I can still take you for a ride."

I shook my head again. "They wouldn't let me do that." I had always wanted to ride in an automobile, but the Dobbses didn't have one, so I thought that meant I never would.

"They don't have to know," he said. I felt his arm slip over my shoulder. My first thought was to brush it off, but for some reason I hesitated. "I can come pick you up tonight after everybody's asleep."

I pulled away from him. "Oh no, I couldn't."

"We wouldn't go far. Just up and down the street. What would that hurt?"

"Well, nothing, I guess, but still, they would—"

"That's right. Wouldn't hurt nothing. I'll pick you up tonight. Say about ten o'clock. Meet me down there at the end of the block so they won't hear the motor."

I started to shake my head, but he reached out and touched my face. "Just trying to cheer you up. That's all."

I was so shocked at the touch of his hand on my face, I couldn't speak. No one had ever touched me that way. It felt nice, but it wasn't like Clarence to be nice, so I felt all mixed up. I watched him as he turned back to the automobile and kept watching him as he drove away. When there was nothing to see but the dust he left, I went back into the house.

"Was that Clarence out there?" Mrs. Dobbs asked.

"Uh-huh."

"What'd he want?"

"I don't know. Something about that saw he loaned Mr. Dobbs."

"His daddy put him up to it, I'd say. Wants to make sure he gets it back. Thinks he can't trust. J. T. I tell you, Clarence's daddy don't think of nobody but hisself."

I didn't answer, but without realizing I was going to, I brought my hand up to my face where Clarence had touched it.

The Dobbses went to bed at their usual time, a little before nine o'clock. I went to my room and blew out the oil lamp like I always did, but I didn't undress and get in bed. The darkness that I usually welcomed after a day of hard work pressed against me with so much heaviness that I had trouble breathing. I could hear a train in the distance. It chugged along like something crippled, and when the whistle blew, it sounded lonesome and mournful. Soon, though, it would be upon us with all its rage and tormented wildness, shaking the house like something having a fit. It's funny that I could usually sleep through all that noise as if it was nothing more than a lullaby, but now it made me want to scream and run away.

I sat there on the edge of the bed, waiting for the noise and the spasms to end, thinking that it was too bad the train came through at nine-twenty instead of ten o'clock so the Dobbses wouldn't hear me when I left.

Nine-twenty. Forty minutes to go. I picked up the alarm clock I kept next to my bed and held it next to the window. There wasn't enough light for me to see clearly, but it looked like no more than a minute had passed. Thirty-nine minutes to go. I didn't dare light the lamp so I could watch the clock, so I counted the minutes away one second at a time the way Davie had taught me so long ago, at about the same time he had taught me to fish.

One-thousand and one, one-thousand and two. . . .

I counted to one thousand and sixty, forty times, keeping count with my fingers by releasing them one at a time from tight fists. When I was done, I got up and tiptoed out the door into the balmy spring night. As it turned out, it was easier than I thought it would be. Neither of them stirred—not even when I stood by the door a while, making up a story about how I couldn't sleep and needed some fresh air. That was just in case one of them got up and looked for me.

When nothing happened, I ran down the front walk and out into the street. It was as dark as a grave all the way down to the end. I stopped running and walked carefully, afraid I would stumble in the darkness. I made it to the end of the street. There was no motor car there waiting for me. There was nothing but the dark shapes of houses looming on each side of the road. No lights shined from their windows.

Maybe I had counted wrong, and I was too early—or too late. Maybe Clarence had given up waiting for me and left. My heart bashed against my chest. I looked down the dark tunnel that was the road, but I saw nothing. No lights. I hoped that meant the Dobbses were still asleep. I turned around and walked into the dark hole that led back to their house, praying I would get inside before either of them awakened.

I'd only taken a few steps when I heard a familiar racket. The front lights of a motor car—I think they're called headlights—moved closer and closer to me. It had to be Clarence. It had to! But if it wasn't, how would I explain to anyone...?

"Well, hello, baby. Sorry I'm late."

"Clarence?"

"Who else was you hoping to meet?"

"Nobody. I just was—"

"Get in. We ain't got all night."

I opened the door—something not all motor cars had—and slid into the seat. Clarence drove away, turning on one of the streets that crossed the railroad tracks to what they called the "good" side of town. I felt a breeze on my face and arms as we moved, and it made me shiver.

"Ain't this fun?" Clarence asked.

"Oh yes," I said, just to be polite. I wasn't at all sure it was fun. I was too worried about being found out, and we were going so fast the bumps in the dirt street made me bounce up and down in the seat.

Clarence turned the car so suddenly I had to hold on to the side of the door to keep from being thrown out the window. That made him laugh.

"Don't be a scaredy-cat," he said.

At least he slowed down, and when we got back to the end of Grove Street where I had waited for him, he stopped the car. When I started to open the door to get out, he reached for me and pulled me toward him.

"What's your hurry?" he asked.

"Well, you know, I'd better not stay out too long. If they find out—"

"They won't find out. Don't be such a wet blanket." He touched my face then, just like he did that other time. My breathing stopped. The next thing I knew his face was so close to mine I could feel his hot breath. "Gimme a kiss," he said. Before I could answer, his lips were on mine.

The kiss didn't last long. Not like it does in a picture show. But it made me feel kind of funny in my stomach all the way down to my legs. Nobody in this world had ever kissed me before.

"Mmmm," he said when he pulled back from me, sounding like he'd just tasted something good. Then he laughed.

"I got to go," I said again.

"Okay," he said. "Can you meet me tomorrow, same time?"

"I better not."

"Suit yourself," he said and drove away. He had stopped the car before we got all the way home, leaving me to enter the dark chasm that led to the Dobbses' house.

15

LOUISA

"How very nice to see you again, my dear," Mrs. Ross said. A maid had just ushered Louisa into the parlor of the house on Third Avenue in the Chestnut Hill District of Richmond. The maid wore a black dress, two shades darker than her skin, and a crisp white apron. Mrs. Ross, Lemuel's mother, sat in the ornate and overly decorated parlor wearing a fashionable dress of muted rose *peau de soie*. She was in her sixties, but the high cheekbones of her face and the alabaster color of her skin hinted of a past beauty, and she still maintained an elegance that commanded attention.

Louisa had come to Richmond to interview a doctor of psychiatry who specialized in treating feebleminded patients. She hoped to get information for her book.

Mrs. Ross rose from her chair and kissed Louisa lightly on her right cheek. Then she motioned with an elegant if heavily veined hand to a chair for Louisa to be seated.

"Lemuel tells me you've been quite busy." Mrs. Ross's voice resonated with an aristocratic southern accent, soothingly soft but with a hint of shadows.

"Oh yes, I have," Louisa said with a little too much enthusiasm. She realized too late that she should have responded with a simple "Yes, ma'am" as a southern girl would have done.

Mrs. Ross smiled faintly. "Writing papers, having them published! Working on a book! So intellectual. So ambitious. So modern!"

Louisa felt uncomfortable. She wasn't sure what was hidden in the shadow of those words. She tried to smile and was grateful for the distraction of the maid walking toward her with a tea cart.

"Would you like tea?" Mrs. Ross asked. Then she added quickly, as if to put Louisa at ease, "Don't be embarrassed, my dear. Ambition is very much admired in young women these days, and I won't add 'not like it was when I was a girl' because that's not necessary, is it? Those days are gone now. Our ambition, I'm afraid, was limited to finding a suitable husband."

Louisa smiled and accepted a cup so delicate and translucent it seemed to be made of ice. The tea inside the cup, though, was dark and steaming.

"You're very brave," Mrs. Ross said as she accepted her own cup. "Writing about epileptics and feebleminded and other deviants. Even women of ill repute."

"Not brave, really," Louisa began before Mrs. Ross interrupted her.

"Oh, of course you are," she said, with a wave of her hand. "I'm sure you had to put yourself in the company of these people, and that takes more courage than I have—or would care to have."

"Yes, ma'am," Louisa said, putting her cup and saucer down as delicately as she could with her shaking hands.

"Forgive me, dear one. I've made you uncomfortable. You're a modern woman. You live in our modern world. Please don't think I'm disturbed by that. My reaction is more awe and curiosity than condemnation."

"You're very kind," Louisa said. She did her best to relax, but she was keenly aware of Mrs. Ross scrutinizing her. Louisa had thought she was prepared for scrutiny and had chosen her wardrobe carefully. She'd eschewed the bright colors that had become so fashionable and wore instead a gray and black dress, made of the new rayon fabric, with a satin sash around the top of her hips. The dress fell just below her knees. Now she thought it was too modern, and the rayon fabric wrinkled too easily. She was suddenly self-conscious of her new hair style, short with marcel wavers. She was even more self-conscious of the beaded band she wore around her hair and forehead.

"I wanted this opportunity to get to know you, Louisa, since each time we've been together we've been in the company of Lemuel. I'm afraid the company of men, no matter how endearing they may be, tends to stifle women to some extent, don't you agree?"

"Certainly," Louisa said with a little laugh that she hoped didn't sound too forced.

"Well, then, tell me about yourself. Oh, I know about you being the only daughter of that very prestigious man and lovely woman in New York, and I know about your interest in educating yourself. Tell me about your work—that paper you wrote and the book you're working on. Something about the minds of perverted women, isn't it?"

"Deviant," Louisa said. "The paper was called 'The Mind of a Deviant Woman.' There is a subtle difference between *perverted* and *deviant*."

Mrs. Ross raised an eyebrow and nodded so slightly that Louisa wasn't certain of the meaning of the gesture. When Mrs. Ross continued looking at her without even picking up her teacup, Louisa continued.

"I chose the word *deviant* because I wanted to look at different circumstances that deviate from the norm. That could include feeblemindedness, epilepsy, prostitution, other forms of low morality, and so forth. There is much discussion among scientists of that sort of thing being hereditary, you see, and I thought it important to look into the minds of people—women in particular since I had to narrow the field—to try to determine how those minds differ."

Mrs. Ross's face had not changed expression, and her eyes had not moved. "And how does a person look into the mind of another?"

A small, nervous laugh escaped Louisa's throat. "I didn't mean that literally, of course. What I meant was I wanted to study deviants. I felt I could do that with interviews and visits, you see. But I only scratched the surface with that little paper. There's much more I want to do."

"Oh, dear," Mrs. Ross said.

"Please don't be alarmed, Mrs. Ross. Psychiatry is a perfectly respectable field."

"Of course it is, Louisa..."

She wanted to add more, Louisa was certain. "But there's more?" she asked, ready for Mrs. Ross's objection that psychiatry was no field for a woman.

"Oh well, it's none of my business at this point, is it?" Mrs. Ross said with a dismissive wave of her hand, leaving Louisa to wonder at what point Mrs. Ross might think it would be her business. Perhaps when she and Lemuel became engaged? "Now, please do have more tea," Mrs. Ross added, "and tell me if you've enjoyed Richmond. I do hope you've had time for pleasure, and it hasn't all been research and work."

"Of course," Louisa said with her best noncommittal smile. The rest of the afternoon was spent talking about such banalities as the historical sites of Richmond and the rest of Virginia, the vagaries of the weather, and the rigors of train travel between New York and Richmond. Although the afternoon had gone much better than Louisa had feared, she was nevertheless happy to leave and meet Lemuel at his office in the late afternoon, as he had requested.

"Oh, hello, darling," Lemuel said, standing up when Louisa was shown in by his secretary. "So, tell me, how was the afternoon with Mother?" He took her hands in both of his and smiled at her.

Louisa was exhausted. She knew she was being tested and scrutinized during tea with Mrs. Ross, and she wasn't at all certain she'd passed the examination. "Well," she said with a little sigh, "I have to confess I was a bit nervous."

"Nonsense." Lemuel brushed her cheek with his lips and led her to one of the comfortable chairs across from his desk, and he sat in another next to her. His office was elaborately furnished, considering he was only a junior partner in the firm. "I'm sure Mother adored you, just as I do," he said. "How could she not?"

His effusiveness made her laugh. "Your mother is very charming," she said, "and lovely. She must have been a real beauty when she was younger."

"Oh yes, she's all of that, but quite open-minded as I'm sure you noticed. I knew the two of you would get along."

Louisa smiled and nodded, hoping he was right. Mrs. Ross had, indeed, been charming and nonjudgmental, and she'd seemed genuinely interested in Louisa and her work.

"I hope you don't mind an early dinner," Lemuel said.

Louisa gave him a smile. "More time to spend with you."

Lemuel laughed uneasily and reached for her hand. "Well, I hope you don't mind sharing me. A couple of my business associates are in town. Both of them are lawyers, of course. We're involved in a case together, and I've asked them to join us. You don't mind, do you?"

"Of course not," Louisa lied, forcing another smile.

Lemuel gave her a quick kiss on the cheek. "You're wonderful," he said, "but my reason for inviting them to join us wasn't entirely selfish on my part. They share your interest in eugenics, and both of them are associated with the Virginia State Colony for Epileptics and Feebleminded. "

Her interest was piqued. "Lemuel, how very sweet of you to think of my interests!"

"I'm very proud of you, darling, and I'll confess, I love showing you off to my friends."

"Showing me off?" Louisa said with a little laugh. "You make me sound like a prized racehorse."

"Don't be ridiculous," Lemuel said, taking her arm. "You're an exceptionally beautiful and intelligent woman, and I love you. That's all that matters."

16

LOUISA

"Irving and Aubrey are both Virginians," Lemuel said when he introduced Irving Whitehead and Aubrey Strode to Louisa as they joined them for dinner. "Irving was a member of the Colony's first board of directors."

"Not sure that was an honor or a curse." Irving's remark, which he made with a knowing smile, brought quiet laughter from Lemuel and his other guest.

"The Colony has had its problems," Aubrey agreed, "but you deserve great credit for overcoming them and launching a fine institution."

Irving gave a dismissive wave of his hand.

"No need to be modest," Lemuel said. "After all, you do have a building on the Colony's campus named for you."

"None of it would have been possible without Aubrey's work," Irving said.

"Aubrey is a former state senator," Lemuel said, turning to Louisa. "His work to benefit the feebleminded and epileptic has been remarkable." He turned to Aubrey. "Heard you may be up for an appointment to the bench."

"And what about you, young man? Rumors that you may be a candidate for the state Senate. . .couldn't choose a better..."

They seemed to go on and on congratulating each other. Louisa lost track of the conversation while she waited for an opportunity to introduce eugenics and hereditary mental defects. She was tired after a stressful day, and for a moment she felt dizzy as the glow from the restaurant's electric lights seemed to dance in front of her.

"Louisa?" Lemuel's voice brought her back suddenly to the moment. "Are you all right?"

"Oh, yes, quite all right," Louisa said with a little laugh.

"You seemed to leave us for a moment," Lemuel said.

"I'm afraid I'm just a bit tired," she said. "Forgive me."

Lemuel chuckled. "She had tea with my mother today. Must have been a little stressful for her. No, don't deny it," he said when he saw she was about to protest. "Mother can be intimidating." He turned to his two friends. "The obligatory visit, you know. Had to make a good impression."

"I'm certain it was no stretch for you to make a good impression, Louisa," Aubrey said. "And no need to let Julia intimidate you. She's a highly accomplished and intelligent woman whom we all admire, but I'm sure you're a match for her."

"Thank you," Louisa said, wondering how Aubrey Strode could know anything at all about her since they'd just met.

"And you will accept the invitation, won't you?" Lemuel asked. Louisa detected something odd in his voice. Irritation? Anxiety?

"Oh...I..." She was acutely embarrassed. She'd lost track of the conversation and had no idea what invitation might have been offered to her.

"I thought you might be interested in visiting the Colony," Irving said.

The Colony. He was speaking of the Virginia Colony for the Epileptic and Feebleminded. "Certainly," she said. "I'd be very interested."

"Thought you would," Irving said, smiling. "I have a confession to make. I read your paper—the one about the minds of women. Very enlightening. Even recommended it to Aubrey here. I was particularly interested in your thoughts about feeblemindedness and heredity," Irving continued. "Not a new concept, of course, but your careful study of mothers and daughters adds credence to the theory."

"I'm afraid I have a long way to go. I just mentioned to Mrs. Ross this afternoon how I've only scratched the surface of the question with that paper."

"You and Mother discussed eugenics?" Lemuel wore an amused expression. "That must have been interesting," he added with another chuckle that sounded condescending.

"Why are you surprised?" Louisa's chagrin was evident in her voice.

There was a moment of silence that could have become embarrassing until Aubrey said, "Ah, the modern woman," and raised his wine glass.

Had she sounded petulant? Too defensive? Louisa wondered.

"I'm interested in that paper Irving mentioned," Aubrey continued. "I've read it myself, and as I said, your ideas on heredity of feeblemindedness and epilepsy are interesting. Why do you say you've only scratched the surface?"

"More study needs to be done—more families, more individuals. But most of all, more depth must be applied to the studies. You've heard of Arthur Estabrook, no doubt? I helped with his studies of degenerate family groups in New York State."

"Oh yes," Aubrey said. "All those mathematical studies that show how many of the children will inherit feeblemindedness and epileptic tendencies when one parent is feebleminded, or when one is not feebleminded but is a so-called carrier, or when both are feebleminded. Get's complicated, doesn't it?"

"It does, Mr. Strode," Louisa said. "And it's all very important, of course, but my interest is in trying to understand the brain—no, the very *mind* of a deviant."

"By interviewing deviants," Aubrey said.

"Exactly."

"A bit risky, isn't it?" Irving asked as he straightened his napkin across his sizable midsection.

"What do you mean?" Louisa asked.

"My dear, deviants don't live in what we consider the safest areas of a city or rural area. They all seem to come from, shall we say, the other side of the tracks."

"That's not necessarily—"

"I find it interesting that you're studying women in particular," Aubrey said, interrupting Louisa. The smile he gave her made his handsome face even more appealing.

"Why yes," Louisa said. "I thought it would be to my advantage to focus on women. I thought perhaps, since I'm a woman, I might be able to better understand the mind of a woman, including a deviant woman."

"Understanding the mind of any woman is a challenge," Lemuel said with a drollness that brought chortles from the other two men.

"Indeed!" Irving said, hefting his glass and spilling a drop or two on the napkin that protected his belly.

They laughed again. All of them except Louisa, who managed a forced smile.

To: Miss Louisa Van Patten, Bryn Mawr College, Pennsylvania
From: Lemuel Ross, Esq., Richmond, Virginia
June 23, 1923

My dear Louisa,

I could not wait another minute to let you know how exceptionally proud I am of you for the way you presented yourself to Aubrey Stroud and Irving Whitehead. I can't stress enough how important the two of them are to the advancement in my career. Your demeanor was almost impeccable in that you demonstrated your considerable intelligence without seeking to show yourself superior to any man. I cannot praise you enough, nor love you enough.

Mother was most impressed with you as well. I know you must be relieved to hear that, since I know you were under some stress meeting with her. It showed on your face.

Mother described you as "an obviously intelligent woman with just enough spirit to be interesting and sufficient good sense not to be too interesting." I am inclined to say that is the way she thinks of herself as well, so I am confident the two of you will get along perfectly. She knows of my intention to present you with an engagement ring in the near future, and although she is far too prudent to admit it outright, I have no doubt that she approves of you in the highest degree.

I am quite busy at the moment, as I am working with Irving on laws regarding the National Farm Loan Policy. I won't bother you with the details since I know you would find them not only difficult to understand, but extremely boring as well. Suffice it to say that the position Irving Whitehead holds with the Federal Intermediate Credit Bank is indeed a prestigious one, and one that Aubrey used his influence to help Irving secure. I might add that it was Irving who saw to it that Aubrey was appointed to the Judge Advocate General's office with the rank of major during the Great War.

Aubrey rose to the rank of colonel, and it was that appointment that set Aubrey on track for his distinguished career as a lawyer and eventually a senator. I know you can see, my dear, how powerful these two men are, how important my relationship with them is, and how important it is that you augment me by making a favorable impression. I want to say again that you did an excellent job of that during dinner. Even the moment when you became a little upset at one of my remarks came across as charming because you were seen as defending my mother.

I must caution you not to work too hard now that you are back at Bryn Mawr. I know your interest in social work among indigents and deviants is important to you, and it is your intellect that drives you, but I implore you to take more time to relax and enjoy yourself. You might even want to consider tempering your goal to become a woman with a profession. I want you to be secure in the knowledge that my career is advancing splendidly, and once you become my wife, you will not have to worry one iota about pursuing a career.

I send you my love and appreciation, and I remain your ever devoted

Lemuel H. Ross, Esq.

17

CARRIE

Clarence kept begging me to go for another ride with him in his car, but I wouldn't do it. I didn't like sneaking out while Mr. and Mrs. Dobbs were asleep. Not just because they could get mad and do something like turn me over to the state, but because it didn't feel right.

"They don't have to know about it," Clarence said.

"Still, it seems like it's not honest," I said.

That made him laugh. "Hell, how can it be dishonest if they don't know about it?" he said.

I didn't know how to answer that.

He started putting his arm around me whenever he could, or he would hold my hand, even in public when he came over to visit with Mr. and Mrs. Dobbs. I can't say I minded a whole lot because, as I said, I liked being touched since nobody ever did it much. The Dobbses looked kind of shocked at first, but after a while they didn't seem to be concerned—not even when Clarence started telling people that I was his girlfriend.

I never thought I'd be anybody's girlfriend, so I was kind of surprised, but I can't say I didn't like the idea of having a boyfriend, even if was just Clarence. I thought Mrs. Dobbs would have a fit over that, but she didn't. She just said at least she could trust Clarence.

The good thing was they said it was all right if I went for a ride in his car, even at night if we went to a picture show. I just loved going to the show, so when he asked me if I wanted to see *Beyond the Rocks*, I said yes because it had Gloria Swanson and Rudolph Valentino in it. I was crazy about both of them. Winona had told me it was about a married woman who falls in love with another man. If the Dobbses had known that, I'm sure they wouldn't have let me go. I didn't tell them, and Clarence didn't mention it either when he came to pick me up.

When he arrived at the house, the minute I opened the door I could smell whiskey on his breath. I'd smelled it on him before, just like I used to smell it on Waverly sometimes, but I didn't say anything. Neither did Mr. or Mrs. Dobbs. They still didn't think Clarence could do anything wrong.

The air was thick with heat and heavy with moisture that July night, and even with the car's open windows, I could feel it pressing down on me. It would be just as hot and uncomfortable inside the theater, but at least I would have the show to help keep my mind off of it. When we got to the end of Grove Street, I expected Clarence to turn the car toward the railroad tracks, so we could cross them and head toward Main Street. Instead, he turned in the opposite direction.

"Where are you going?" I asked.

All he said was "You'll see."

"I thought we were going to see *Beyond the Rocks.*"

If I sounded disappointed, he didn't seem to care. He just laughed and said he had something better than a picture show in mind.

He drove out to that same spot where he had first kissed me and stopped the car. We had been to that spot a few more times, and he always wanted to kiss me and fondle my breasts. I really didn't enjoy that too much, not nearly as much as going to a picture show or as much as a gentle touch on my face the way he did it that time. This time, though, instead of reaching for me and putting his hands and mouth all over me, he got out of the car and pulled a quilt out of the back. Then he opened the door on my side, took my hand, and pulled me out.

"What are you doing?" I asked.

"You sure ask a lot of questions," he said as he spread the quilt on the ground. "Come here," he added, trying to pull me down onto the quilt.

I pulled back. "I don't want to. I want to go to the picture show."

"Sit down. Don't you want to look at the stars?"

"It's too hot."

"No it ain't." He tugged at my hand. It was a gentle tug, and he smiled up at me. "Come on, honey, just sit here with me for a little while. We got plenty of time before the picture show starts."

"Well, okay," I said, settling down beside him, "but I'm not in the mood for no kissing."

He laughed. "I won't kiss you if you don't want me to."

He was rubbing my back, and it felt good. When he lay down on the quilt and pulled me down with him, it was such a gentle pull that I couldn't resist, and I found myself lying beside him. We were facing each other, and he moved toward me. Before I knew it, he was kissing me on the lips, even though he said he wouldn't do that. I didn't resist. It really wasn't too bad. When his hands started moving all over me, going inside my dress and pulling at my nipples, I didn't try to stop him. I just thought that maybe he would get tired of it pretty soon, and we could go to the picture show.

All of a sudden he rolled on top of me, and he was kissing me so hard it made my mouth hurt. I tried to cry out, but my cry was muffled by his mouth, so I pushed at him and tried to tell him to get off of me. Finally he rolled off on his back.

"You were hurting me!" I was doing my best not to cry.

He didn't answer me. He just lay there breathing hard. I started to get up, but he pulled me down again. He started kissing me again, and his hands were exploring my body the way they'd done before. He reached under my dress and, with a quick tug, pulled my underwear down.

"Clarence, no. I don't want you to. . ."

His finger was inside me, massaging me, and it scared me.

"You're wet," he said. "You want it, don't you?"

I tried to tell him no, but he was lying on top of me again, forcing the breath from my lungs with the top of his body. I couldn't tell what he was doing at first, but in the next moment, I knew he was unbuttoning his pants. He released the pressure from my chest as he forced himself inside me.

"No!" I said. "No, I don't want—"

"Just shut up and enjoy it," he said, pumping on top of me, hurting me. I closed my eyes and prayed it would end soon.

He let out a loud groan and collapsed his body on top of me, pressing me into the ground. I could feel his sweat, mingled with mine, sticky and wet against our bare stomachs. My body was jerking with sobs like somebody having a falling fit. Finally, he rolled off of me.

"Now what are you blubbering about?" he asked, still breathing hard.

"What you did," I said, sobbing. "I didn't want...It was wrong. You never should have—"

"Wrong? What was wrong with it?"

"It's fornicating. We can go to hell for that."

"Then there's going to be a lot of people in hell," he said, rubbing my back again. "Everybody does it."

"But if you're not married, it's a sin."

"No it ain't. But even if it is, I ain't going to stop doing it."

"What if you got me pregnant?"

He laughed. "You ain't never done it with anybody before, have you? You can't get pregnant the first time you do it."

"What if that's not true? What if you can get pregnant the first time?"

He laughed again. "Don't worry about it, honey. I'm gonna marry you anyway."

That almost knocked the breath out of me as much as his heavy body on top of me had. "Marry me?" I finally managed to say.

"Sure," he said and reached for me. "Come on, let's do it again."

"No," I said. "I don't want to. I want to go to the picture show."

He kept begging me to let him do it again, and I kept saying no. This time I stood up so he couldn't roll on top of me, and I was ready to run if he came at me. After a while he gave up, and we went to the show. I don't remember anything about it, even though it was one I'd been wanting to see for a long time. All I could do was sit there and cry and do my best not to let Clarence or anybody else around us know.

It wasn't until the next morning that I saw the blood on my underwear and even on the inside of my thighs. I hadn't seen it the night before since I didn't want to light a lamp and risk waking up Mr. and Mrs. Dobbs. At first I thought it was a good sign, that it meant I was getting my period early and that there was no way I could be pregnant if I was bleeding.

I felt different on the inside though—like a part of me had been stolen. I was half afraid that it showed on the outside, that Mrs. Dobbs would be able to tell just by looking at me what had happened to me.

I didn't want to be alone with Clarence anymore. I hoped I'd get to where I wouldn't feel that way eventually, since I was going to be his wife. He did come around several times, but I always managed to come up with an excuse not to go with him. That really wasn't too hard because Mrs. Dobbs kept me busy in the house and in the garden. All the work, along with the heat, made me feel extra tired.

There were a few times when I couldn't come up with an excuse, and I ended up going out with him. He always wanted me to do it with him again, but I told him no. I said I would tell everybody that he raped me if he made me do it again. That seemed to scare him enough that he quit trying to get me to do it. He even quit coming around so much.

A few weeks after it happened, I started to fear that I was pregnant. I was a week late starting my period, and I'd never been that late before. I thought maybe I was late because I had already shed a little bit of blood that night Clarence did it to me. By the time I was two weeks late, I knew that wasn't that case, although it was almost a year before I found out what that blood really was that showed up after Clarence made me do it. Before long I was sick and throwing up in the morning. I knew what that meant. I'd heard Lucy talking about her morning sickness. I knew I had to tell Clarence as soon as possible so we could get married before the Dobbses found out about my condition.

The next time he came around, I told him I wanted to go for a ride out in the country the way we used to do. That made him happy. He could hardly wait to get me out there.

When we got to the spot with all the trees where we'd gone before, he stopped the car. Before he could get out, I reached for his arm to stop him. He gave me a surprised look.

"I got something to tell you," I said.

"What?" He was frowning, and he looked kind of anxious.

"We got to get married right away. I'm pregnant."

He turned white and didn't say anything for a while. Finally he said, "No you ain't."

I nodded and whispered, "I am."

He turned even whiter before he got out and cranked the car to start the motor again. Then he got in and drove me back to the Dobbses' place without saying another word.

18

CARRIE

It seemed I was managing not to let Mrs. Dobbs know that I was sick every morning. It had always been my practice to get up before anyone else so I could get the fire going in the stove in the kitchen to cook breakfast. Now I got up even earlier so I could race outside to the outhouse, throw up, and get back to the house in time to wash my face. She did notice that I was tired most of the time.

"What's wrong with you, girl? You gettin' lazy?" she asked me over and over again. I always told her I wasn't lazy, that I was just a little tired. At that time, I didn't know that being pregnant could make you feel tired.

I went to bed as early as I could every night, and I still believed she didn't suspect anything. I just kept wishing Clarence would come by and tell me when we were going to get married. I hoped it would be soon. Weeks and weeks went by, however, and I didn't see him. He had just stopped coming by like he used to do.

It was late September but still as hot as summer, and I was in the kitchen doing the ironing. It was extra hot in the house because I had to keep a fire in the stove to heat the irons. Sweat was rolling off of me, making my limbs sticky and my hair look like a wet mop. By this time, I was growing in the middle and in my breasts, so my clothes were too tight, and that, along with the heat, made me feel like I was going to pass out.

I had the window open, but there was no breeze. There was nothing but hot, syrupy September. I was glancing out the window, hoping for some sign of a little wind to stir the leaves of the willow tree, when I heard a familiar rattling sound and saw Clarence drive up in his car.

My heart skipped a beat. He had come at last! I watched as he got out of the car and made his way over to the spot under the willow tree where Mr. Dobbs was sitting in his chair, fanning himself with a folded newspaper. They talked for a few minutes, and I dared to hope that Clarence was telling him he'd come to get me to marry him. The next thing I knew, Clarence was walking back to his car.

I had to do something fast.

Placing the flatiron back on the stove, I hurried out the door. Clarence saw me. I know he did. But he didn't wave or even look at me. Instead, he looked away as quick as he could, acting like he hadn't seen me, and sped away, stirring up a fog of dust.

I stood there watching him, feeling like somebody had hit me in the stomach. All of a sudden, I was aware of Mr. Dobbs watching me.

"That was Clarence," I said because I couldn't think of anything else to say.

"It was," he said. He looked at me for a few seconds and chuckled. "Didn't stick around long, did he? I thought he said you was his girlfriend."

I didn't answer. I just watched Clarence's car disappear in that ugly curtain of dust.

Mr. Dobbs chuckled again. "Well, I guess that's a boy for ya, huh?"

Then it happened one morning several weeks later. When I got up, Mrs. Dobbs was sitting in the kitchen, waiting for me.

"Sit down, Carrie. I want to talk to you," she said.

"Excuse me, but I got to go to the—."

"I said sit down!"

The sound of her voice scared me. She made me work hard, but she hardly ever raised her voice that way. I sat down. My stomach churned, and I started to feel woozy like I was going to faint. I jumped up as fast as I could and barely made it out the door before I started retching, right there on the back step. I hadn't thrown up in a long time. I thought that part of carrying a baby was over, but there it was again.

Finally, I went back into the house feeling weak, like I could hardly stand up. "I'm sorry," I said. "I'll clean it up. I guess I must have ate—"

"Don't give me no lies, Carrie. I know you're pregnant."

I had never seen her eyes look so cold or her face look so much like a stone. I didn't know what to say

"I see your belly and your breasts. You've shamed this family," she said. "I don't know how you could of done that to us after all we done for you."

"I never meant to bring you shame, and it wasn't my—"

"I don't want no excuses. I thought I could trust you, but I should of knowed better, you bein' that woman's daughter."

I ducked my head, wishing I could get out of that kitchen, but she just kept on. "You shamed Clarence, too. I think he was gettin' sweet on you, but I can tell you nobody, not Clarence or nobody, is goin' to want damaged goods."

"But, ma'am, it was him that—"

"I'll have to talk this over with J. T. Now you get that mess out there cleaned up before it dries."

"Yes, ma'am," I said to her back as she left the room. Part of me wanted to yell at the top of my lungs that it was Clarence who did this to me and it was by force. Another part, the part that won out in the end, just wanted to hang my head in shame and try not to think about it anymore. That was impossible. I had to think about it.

I was scared. When Mrs. Dobbs said she'd have to talk to Mr. Dobbs about it, I knew that whatever they decided wouldn't be good for me. My only hope was that Clarence would show up again and keep his promise to marry me. Not that I thought it would be such a good life being married to Clarence, but I didn't think it would be much worse that living with the Dobbses. And now that I was pregnant, it had to be a whole lot better.

I went up to my room early that night, just as I always did, but this time I didn't get in bed. Instead I waited a little while and then tiptoed to the top of the stairs, staying in the shadows so I could hear Mr. and Mrs. Dobbs talking without them seeing me.

"You sure?" Mr. Dobbs said.

"Of course I'm sure. I thought I seen her gettin' up and going outside to puke for several mornings a while back. Now she's gettin' a belly on her, and her breasts is fillin' out. Besides that, I can tell by the way she's actin'. Tired all the time. That's the way you are the first few months."

"Well, maybe she just ate something that don't agree with her."

"Good Lord, J. T., it ain't something she ate. She's pregnant. She as much as admitted it."

"Well then, who done it to her? Wasn't Clarence, was it? Because if it was--"

"J. T., it don't matter who done it to her. We can't let her stay here now. Think of what folks will say. And you don't really think Clarence would do something like that, do you? My own sister's son?"

After that, nobody said anything for several seconds. Finally, I heard Mr. Dobbs clear his throat. "All right then, I'll talk to Judge Shackelford about it, see what we can do."

"Judge Shackelford? Ain't that the judge that had Emma committed?"

"It is, Alice," Mr. Dobbs said.

"I think that's a good idea, J. T. A real good idea."

To: Miss Louisa Van Patten, Bryn Mawr College
From: Mrs. Alice Harris, District Nurse
Charlottesville, Virginia
November 1923

My dearest Louisa,

I was so immensely delighted to receive the news in your last letter of your engagement to Lemuel Ross! Didn't I tell you that I was certain he would pop the question? A man would be a fool not to realize what a tremendous asset you would be to him as a wife. You seemed greatly relieved that his mother was so approving of the match, but I must say that doesn't surprise me either. You are a charming and gracious woman who would never embarrass his family. How could she help but approve?

Yes, of course, I would be more than happy to receive an invitation to the wedding. You have only to let me know when and where, and I shall be there. You did mention that the date has yet to be set, but it won't be long, I'm sure. You must be ecstatic since Lemuel Ross is so very well known in Virginia and so successful in his law firm, not to mention all the talk about him as a possible governor! What will be next? The presidency? Don't laugh or scold. I know I'm getting ahead of myself, but he has quite a favorable reputation here in Virginia, as you must know.

I am certain that you have more than enough to keep you occupied while you wait to set a wedding date, namely the work on your book and your potential career interests. I am not one of those old-fashioned women who condemn you for your interests. Education never hurt anyone, and I know how fulfilling a career can be.

That brings me to the second reason for writing to you. Knowing of your interest in studying the minds of deviant women, particularly in regard to hereditary characteristics, I thought of you immediately when new developments arose in the Emma Buck case.

In this instance, the new development involves Emma's daughter Carrie, whom I believe you have met.

Carrie's guardians, Mr. and Mrs. J. T. Dobbs, have petitioned the courts to have Carrie committed to the Virginia State Colony for Epileptics and Feebleminded in Madison Heights. As I'm sure you remember, that is where her mother, Emma, now resides. It appears they are claiming the girl is incorrigible and given to hysteria, epilepsy, hallucinations, and feeblemindedness. They have stated that they saw these symptoms shortly after they agreed to take her as their ward, but that the symptoms have worsened. They are now physically and financially unable to continue to care for her.

As you no doubt know, the wheels of justice turn oh so slowly, and the hearing will not be held until the calendar turns to a new year. It is scheduled for January 23, 1924, in the judge's chambers here in Charlottesville. (How strange it is to be writing 1924 already. It's hard to believe the new century has been almost one quarter lived!)

If you should find yourself able to attend the hearing, I feel certain that you can be afforded the opportunity to interview Carrie either before or after the proceedings. As Judge Shackelford, who will be in charge, is a close friend, I am comfortable in assuring you that I can *guarantee* the opportunity. Indeed, what a wonderful chance it will be for you to have yet another set of feebleminded, deviant women to add to your study cases. I am so immensely enthusiastic about your work and so impressed with your intellect, I want to do everything within my power to aid you.

I, of course, expect to be at the hearing. I do so look forward to seeing you again.

Your devoted friend,
Alice Harris, RN

P.S. You asked me about Ben Newman, who has an interest in the eugenics movement. I'm afraid I don't know him at all, but as I'm

sure you know, our numbers are growing exponentially so it is difficult to meet everyone. You mentioned that he is a journalist which
would make it even more unlikely that I would know him. However,
if I may offer a word of caution: It is always best to avoid journalists.

A. H.

19

CARRIE

They thought I didn't know what was going on when they told me we had to go down to the courthouse to talk to a judge. I knew it meant they were going to try to have me committed someplace. The only place I knew of that people got sent to when they got committed was the Colony where they sent Mama. But that was for feebleminded people and people with epilepsy. I wasn't feebleminded, and I didn't have epilepsy, so I didn't know where they'd try to send me. Not an orphanage. I was too old for that.

It was cold that day with snow falling down from an invisible sky, the way the Bible says mana came down for the children of Israel. I was scared as we walked toward the courthouse with all of its glass eyes staring at me. Once inside, it was stuffy hot, and we walked upstairs to an office that had a sign on the door telling us it was the Office of the Honorable Charles D. Shackelford. It was even hotter up there on the second floor. When Mr. Dobbs opened the door for me and Mrs. Dobbs, I was surprised to see that pretty woman, Miss Louisa Van Patten, along with that nurse. I think her name was Anne Harris. Mama had told me who they were after I'd seen them talking to her that time down by the grocery store. That was some time ago.

Miss Van Patten smiled at me, and I smiled back while the one in the nurse's uniform kept checking things in a notebook. Miss Van

Patten had changed her style of dress. She looked very modern in a dark-blue dress with a straight skirt and a bodice that dropped below her waist. I knew all about the new fashions because I looked through the magazines in the drugstore when I got the chance. My own dress was out of style with its full sleeves and a belt at the waist, which I had started leaving unfastened because of my growing middle.

"Oh, hello," the nurse said, looking up when she realized we had come into the room. "You are Mr. and Mrs. Dobbs? And Carrie?" she added, looking at me.

Mr. Dobbs mumbled something I couldn't understand, and he had a suspicious frown on his face. The nurse introduced herself and Miss Van Patten as well. She went on to say that she knew we were there to see the judge, but she wondered if the two of them could have a few minutes to talk to me after the hearing.

"Talk to Carrie?" Mr. Dobbs said. I could tell he was wary of her. "What about?"

"Medical reasons," Nurse Harris said.

"Medical reasons? The judge already had her checked over by that Dr. Flippen. We had to take her to see him and Dr. Coulter both. Dr. Coulter's our family doctor."

"I understand, sir. This is for reasons of mental health."

"They both already said she was feebleminded."

Feebleminded? That got my attention. Nobody ever said before that I was feebleminded, and I didn't see how those two doctors would know that since I barely said anything to them. I had been too scared to talk much.

"You a nurse?" Mr. Dobbs asked. He was eyeing her uniform.

"I'm the district nurse for Albemarle County. I wrote you a letter once regarding Mrs. Emma Buck."

"Oh, so that was you," Mr. Dobbs said. "And what did you say her name was?" He pointed at Miss Van Patten.

"Miss Louisa Van Patten. She's assisting me. And I might add that Judge Shackelford has given us permission to speak with Carrie."

"Well, in that case, I guess it's all right," Mr. Dobbs said, but he sounded like he wasn't sure it really was all right.

"Oh, thank you," the nurse said. "We won't bother you now because I know you'll be called into the judge's chambers shortly, but if we could have a few moments with Carrie after your meeting, I would appreciate it. We'll speak to her in my office just down the hall."

Mr. Dobbs nodded and was about to sit down, but before he made contact with the chair, a woman came out and said, "Judge Shackelford will see you now in his courtroom. Miss Harris, Miss Van Patten, you may enter as well."

I was about to follow the Dobbses into the courtroom when Miss Van Patten surprised me by saying she hoped I didn't mind taking the time to talk to her afterward. I was so surprised that I didn't know what to say. I wasn't used to people asking me if I minded or if I didn't mind. It turned out I didn't have to say anything because Mr. Dobbs answered for me.

"She don't mind if that's what it takes," he said. "Now come on, Carrie; let's get this over with."

I followed them into the courtroom, wishing with all of my soul that I didn't have to go in there.

The wood paneling in that big room reminded me of a dark forest in the winter when there's nothing green to be seen. There were photographs of old men on the walls, all gray and black, and there was a big desk the color of dry lichen. A man wearing a black suit sat behind a tall desk, and the two doctors who had examined me sat at a long table. Along one side of the room there was a row of windows that showed nothing but the colorless sky and a few bare tree branches outside. Miss Van Patten and Nurse Harris sat on benches facing the judge.

The man behind the desk didn't look at either Mrs. Dobbs or me. It was to Mr. Dobbs that he spoke.

"Morning, J. T."

"Morning, Judge. This here's my wife. You met her when we taken in the girl."

"Miz Dobbs," he said, nodding at her. "Y'all have a seat, and this hearing will commence."

He started reading from a piece of paper that he had on the desk in front of him. His voice reminded me of a bee buzzing, just going on and on and on without any expression at all. It made it hard to pay attention. I did catch the words that this was a hearing to see if one Carrie Buck was feebleminded and if she was a suitable subject for an institution. The way it sounded to me was like he was talking about someone else. Maybe that's because except for that one time when he called me "one Carrie Buck," he always just said "the girl," like maybe he was talking about somebody who wasn't sitting there in front of him.

Finally he stopped reading and spoke to the two doctors.

"I examined the girl as you requested, and I have concluded that she is feebleminded," the one called Dr. Flippen said.

I felt my stomach turn over when he said that. I still couldn't figure out why he would think such a thing when he hadn't spent much time at all with me, and I hadn't said more than three words to him because I was too scared to speak. Then Dr. Coulter said the same thing—that I was feebleminded. Said it with me sitting right there in front of him and him knowing it wasn't true. I had only seen him once before, back when I cut my finger all the way to the bone when a knife slipped as I was cooking. That was a long time ago, and I remember him saying I was a strong girl for my age and he was glad to know I was doing so well in school. And I was. I was getting good report cards back then.

When it came time for Mr. Dobbs to talk, he answered questions about when and where I was born and who my mama was. He also told the judge my daddy's name was Frank Buck, and he was dead, killed in some kind of accident. That was the same thing Mama had told me.

"How long have you had the girl in your care?" the judge asked.

"Since 1909," Mr. Dobbs said. "I believe she was about three years old then."

"Did the girl go to school?" the judge asked.

"Oh yes," Mr. Dobbs said. "We sent her to school. We wanted to do the right thing for her, don't you know."

"And she learned to read and write?"

"Oh yes," Mr. Dobbs said. "She could read and write good as anybody."

"She is able to recognize and distinguish objects?" the judge asked.

"Yes sir," Mr. Dobbs said. I saw him glance at Mrs. Dobbs and saw the look she gave him. "But...but I would say she weren't able to, you know, take proper notice of things," he added.

"Can you explain that please? That she wasn't able to take proper notice of things?"

"Well, by that I mean she wasn't, you know, quite right." Mr. Dobbs glanced at his wife again. "She was, well, peculiar," he said, looking at the judge. "It was something she was born with, I guess. Her mama's feebleminded, you know. She's in the Colony."

"The Virginia State Colony for Epileptics and Feebleminded, you mean."

"Yes sir. And...and I would say the girl's probably got epilepsy."

I couldn't believe he said that, but I saw Mrs. Dobbs smile and nod.

"What makes you believe she has epilepsy?" the judge asked.

Mr. Dobbs looked nervous. He looked at his wife again, took a handkerchief out of his pocket, and wiped his forehead. "Well, she has them fits. You know what I mean. Them epileptic fits. Especially when she was little."

"I see," the judge said.

But I didn't see. I didn't see how Mr. Dobbs could say such a thing because I'd never had an epileptic fit in my life.

"All right," the judge said. "How about her moral character?"

"Her what?" Mr. Dobbs looked confused, and he glanced at Mrs. Dobbs again. "Oh, morals. Uh, I'd say not good."

"Not good?" The judge frowned at him. "Do you mean she's morally delinquent?"

"Yes sir. That's it. That's what I mean."

"Thank you, Mr. Dobbs," the judge said. "Mrs. Dobbs," he said, turning to her, "I'd like to ask you a few questions."

Mrs. Dobbs didn't look as nervous as Mr. Dobbs had been, but she didn't look at me. In fact, it seemed that she was doing all she could not to look at me.

The judge asked her some of the same questions about how old I was when I went to live with them, how old I was now, and if I went to school.

"Oh, she went to school. I seen to that," Mrs. Dobbs said. "But she wasn't no good at any of her subjects."

"Not good at any of her subjects? I've seen her report cards, Mrs. Dobbs. It appears she did average or above in most of her subjects." The judge was once again looking down at the papers on his desk.

Mrs. Dobbs squirmed in her chair. "Well, I guess I misunderstood you, judge. What I mean is she didn't have a good attitude. She was always disagreeable, and she had temper tantrums."

The judge looked up from his desk to Mrs. Dobbs. "Describe her tantrums."

"She'd pout sometimes when things didn't go her way. And have fits, you know."

"Fits? Do you mean epileptic fits?"

"Yes. Yes, that's what I mean," Mrs. Dobbs said.

I nearly came out of my chair because here was that lie again, but I forced myself to hold still.

"Uh-huh," the judge said and looked down at the papers on his desk again. "Now, as to her epilepsy, when did you first notice it?"

"When she was, oh, I would say, maybe ten years old. She had these headaches, see, and then she'd have a nervous fit."

"Nervous fit? Do you mean convulsions?"

Mrs. Dobbs frowned, making me think she didn't know what he meant by convulsions. She never did say anything; she just nodded her head.

"Can you describe the epileptic symptoms more fully?"

"Well, I would say that she...well, I can't exactly say."

"You can't say? Do you mean you can't remember?" the judge asked.

"Well…" Mrs. Dobbs didn't say anything for several seconds. "I can't remember it too much. Them, you know, symptoms, as you say."

"How about the headaches and convulsions? Do you remember anything about them?"

"I…I can't say that I do." It seemed to me that Mrs. Dobbs was getting scared. Maybe she didn't want to get caught in too many lies for fear they'd put *her* in the Colony.

"Mrs. Dobbs, do you still contend that Carrie Buck is feebleminded?"

Mrs. Dobbs brightened and sat up straighter. It was like she was glad the judge was finally saying something she could understand. "There's no doubt in my mind but what she's feebleminded."

"It is my understanding that Miss Buck is unmarried and is expecting a child."

"That is right, Your Honor."

The judge pushed the papers on his desk aside and looked straight at Mrs. Dobbs. "Mrs. Dobbs, if Carrie is sent to the Colony, she will be expected to be able to protect herself against ordinary dangers without an attendant. By ordinary dangers, I mean such things as avoiding harm to herself when cooking or walking or fetching something from a high shelf or even defending herself from an attacker, within reason. Otherwise, she is not a suitable candidate for the Colony. Do you understand?"

Now Mrs. Dobbs looked as nervous as Mr. Dobbs had looked a few minutes earlier. She answered simply, "Yes sir."

"Would you say, then, that Carrie Buck is capable of protecting herself against ordinary dangers without an attendant?"

"Yes sir." Mrs. Dobbs sounded kind of uncertain. It wasn't that she didn't know the answer. It was more that she was afraid she wouldn't give the judge the answer he wanted.

The judge turned to me. "Carrie, do you have anything to say at this point?"

I wanted with everything in my soul to say that I'd never had any epileptic fit in my life, and I wanted to tell him about that note I got from Miss Nelson that said "very good in deportment and lessons." I couldn't make any sound come out of my throat though. I was just too nervous. All I could do was shake my head as if to say no.

The judge nodded. He picked up some papers from his desk and spent several minutes looking at them. I couldn't stand to look at him, and I couldn't look at either Mr. or Mrs. Dobbs. All I could do was stare in front of me without seeing anything. It seemed to take forever before the judge spoke again.

"After reviewing reports from two physicians, hearing the testimony of Mr. and Mrs. J. T. Dobbs, observing Carrie Buck, and taking note that she is the daughter of a prostitute and that she herself is unmarried and pregnant, I have determined that Carrie Buck is a suitable subject to be admitted to an institution for the care and treatment of the feebleminded. I therefore order her to be delivered to the superintendent of the Virginia State Colony for Epileptics and Feebleminded without further delay."

20

CARRIE

I thought for a minute that the judge had made a mistake. He must have meant to say something else because I knew I wasn't feebleminded and didn't have epilepsy. But those words kept pounding in my head. *Colony...without delay.*

Someone, I'm not sure who, pulled me from my chair and led me into the hallway. Was it Miss Van Patten? Was Nurse Harris walking with us? I think both must have been there. I think Miss Van Patten showed me into an office and asked me questions. What did she ask? What did I answer? All I can remember hearing were those words: *Colony...without delay.*

"Get your things together," Mrs. Dobbs said when the two women were finished with their questioning and I was back at the Dobbses' house. "You'll be leaving soon. By tomorrow, I reckon."

I know she was anxious to get rid of me for a lot of reasons. One was that Lucy was expecting again, and the baby was due about the same time as my baby was supposed to be born. Mrs. Dobbs was planning to go to Lovingston to help Lucy when her baby came. But Mr. Dobbs said I wouldn't be leaving tomorrow. He said papers had to be sent to the welfare office, and it would be at least a week and maybe longer. I couldn't tell if that disappointed Mrs. Dobbs or not. She made the best of it, though, and sent me to the kitchen to make biscuits for dinner. I didn't mind because I thought that would help me keep my mind off of what had just happened. It didn't. I guess I'd made so many biscuits over the past ten or eleven years, since I was six years old, that I just did it without thinking, and that left my mind open to think about other things.

I wondered what it would be like at the Colony. Would I get to be with Mama? What would I do there? Would I have my baby there? If it was a girl, I was going to name her Annabelle. Would I be able to keep Annabelle with me? How long would I be there? Not long, I hoped. I sure didn't want to raise Annabelle in that place.

Thinking about Annabelle was something I liked to do, so I pushed the thought of the Colony out of my mind and started wondering what color Annabelle's eyes would be and whether or not she would look like me or like Clarence. I hoped she would look like me. Not that Clarence wasn't a nice-looking boy. It was just that I didn't want to be reminded of him. Even if I had a boy, I didn't want him to look like Clarence. But I wouldn't have a boy. Somehow I knew that.

A week passed, and we still hadn't heard anything about me going to the Colony. Another week passed, and before I knew it, it was February, and a whole month had gone by. Mr. Dobbs said he guessed he'd have to look into it. Mrs. Dobbs said it was embarrassing to her that I was getting so big with everybody knowing I wasn't married. I didn't think much about being embarrassed because all I could think about was how my back hurt and how hard it was to sleep at night, especially when Annabelle would try to stick her elbow or her heel through my womb, and I kept having to get up to pee.

"Goddamned red tape," Mr. Dobbs said when he came home one day in early March, about six weeks before Annabelle was due. "I checked with the welfare office, and the papers has been tied up because somebody didn't fill 'em out right and then didn't even take care of it when they was sent back to be fixed."

"Well, they better get the papers fixed soon," Mrs. Dobbs said. "I got to go to Lovingston just any day now." Usually she would scold Mr. Dobbs for cussing, but she didn't this time. I think she probably felt like cussing, too.

"I know, I know." Mr. Dobbs sounded like he was running out of patience. "One of them Red Cross nurses told me she was the one that wrote to the welfare office, and she told 'em we had to get Carrie in the Colony before the baby comes."

So Annabelle would be born in the Colony. At least I knew now, but I wasn't sure how I felt about it. The Colony didn't seem like a very good place to be born, but on the other hand, if I didn't go there, I'd end up having her at home, and Mrs. Dobbs wouldn't like that. I didn't want Annabelle to be someplace where she wasn't wanted.

It was the twentieth of March, and Mrs. Dobbs was fit to be tied. She was going on the train to Lovingston in two more days so she'd be there when Lucy's baby came, and I was still at home, no more than three weeks before Annabelle was supposed to be born.

"That's the gov'ment for you. Can't do anything right, don't care how much they put you out or leave you hanging." Mrs. Dobbs was packing her suitcase to get on the train the next day, fussing and fuming the whole time. When she got done with the government, she turned on me. "If you hadn't gone and got yourself in trouble, I wouldn't have this to worry about. Shoulda knowed I couldn't trust you, you being the daughter of a whore. Well, that's what I get for trying to be a good Christian, I guess."

It surprised both of us when Mr. Dobbs came home from work early that day. Mrs. Dobbs had just put her suitcase next to the front door when he came in the back.

"What are you doing here?" she asked when she saw him.

"Thought I better show you this," he said, pulling a paper out of his vest pocket.

"You got word about Carrie?" Mrs. Dobbs sounded excited.

"It's a letter from Arthur Priddy." Mr. Dobbs was unfolding the paper.

"Who's that?"

"Superintendent of the Colony." He handed the letter to Mrs. Dobbs.

"No, you read it to me," she said. "I swear, my nerves is so frazzled I don't think I could make heads or tails of it." I don't think she realized I was still in the room. Usually, she sent me out to the kitchen when she had something to talk about with Mr. Dobbs.

Mr. Dobbs squinted at the letter. "Well, it's addressed to that woman at the Red Cross that's been trying to help us. She gave me this copy. It says, 'My dear Miss Wilhelm, I have your letter of the eleventh, relative to the admission of Carrie E. Buck and note that you say she is expecting her baby around—'"

"Skip that part," Mrs. Dobbs said. "What does it say about when Carrie's leaving?"

Mr. Dobbs mumbled to himself as he read through the parts of the letter Mrs. Dobbs didn't want to hear. Then he began reading aloud. "'I am sorry, but we make it a rule to positively refuse admission of any expectant mother to the Colony. You will have to make provisions to keep her until the child is born and disposed of, and then we will take her when the law has been complied with in committing her. I have advised Mr. Richey that he will have to send me a copy of the warrant on which she was committed. Very truly, A. S. Priddy, Superintendent.'"

"Well, my Lord," Mrs. Dobbs said. She sounded like she was about to cry. If she said anything else, I didn't hear it because I ran out of the room.

I didn't like that man who wrote the letter calling my baby "it." She was a human being growing inside me, and her name would be Annabelle. And what did he mean by her being disposed of?

To: Lemuel Ross, Richmond, Virginia
From: Louisa Van Patten, Bryn Mawr College
July 31, 1923

Dearest Lemuel,

I must say I was surprised at your response to my letter in which I wrote you about my interview with Carrie Buck and explained how much insight I gained regarding her condition. I thought you would understand my aroused interest at seeing that she was so detached and unresponsive, indicating feeblemindedness, and how it seems so obvious that she has inherited the condition from her mother.

Perhaps I was too enthusiastic in my description of the interview and how it enhanced my comprehension of the subject that interests me. Perhaps, also, I should not have mentioned that I hope to interview her again in the near future. I did not expect that to upset you. I cannot deny my enthusiasm for my work, but I do deny your accusation that my career is of more importance to me than you, your career, and our future together. Yes, I do admit that I did not mention our wedding in my last missive, but it is still months away, my love, as you know. Do not we each have much on our mind to occupy us in the meantime? I personally think it is a good thing that we have such full and mind-enriching lives. It makes us more interesting individuals, don't you agree?

I was dismayed to hear of your mother's recent illness, and I have sent her a note wishing her a speedy recovery. I was happy to hear that she expressed to you her desire to see me again soon, and I assure you that I conveyed my own ardent wish to see her in the letter I sent. In response to your inquiry, I assure you that, yes, I will keep her abreast of all of the wedding plans, and I have conveyed the same to her. You are correct that responsibility for the "production," as you called it, falls to the bride's family, but I urge you to rest comfortably in the knowledge that my mother excels

---

at this sort of thing, and nothing can possibly go awry. She is very aware of the "important personages" you mentioned who will be attending the wedding as guests of your family. She is quite used to my father fretting over the politicians and other people of note he is obliged to impress in his own career. Therefore, I urge you not to worry. All is well and in good hands.

I do so very much look forward to seeing you again when next I am in Richmond. I give you my word that I will spend as much time as possible with you and will not go scurrying off too soon to do more research for my project. However, I know you will understand when I ask you please not to refer to it as my "ridiculous little" project, as it is very important to me.

You must relax more, my dear, and rest in the assurance that I will soon be Mrs. Lemuel Ross and know that in the meantime I am

Your faithful and loving,
Louisa

21

CARRIE

I was bringing a five-gallon bucket of water in from the pump outside the kitchen when my water broke. I set the bucket down on the ground and ran into the house because I knew what was happening.

"What'd you do? Spill that whole bucket of water?" Mrs. Dobbs asked when she saw how wet I was. She had just come back from Lovingston since Lucy's baby had come earlier than expected. She'd been complaining all day about how tired she was. It wasn't more than a second, though, before she put both of her hands to her mouth and said, "Lord have mercy, your water broke!"

She made me lie down on my bed, and she went next door to tell the neighbor to call the doctor. The neighbors had just put in a telephone, which seemed like a handy thing to have.

I tried to be still like Mrs. Dobbs told me, but it was impossible to keep myself lying flat on the bed because I started having pains. They weren't too bad at first, but in a little while, one came like a wave over my whole body, hurting so bad that I sat straight up and then doubled over.

"Stay down!" Mrs. Dobbs said. She stayed with me until the doctor got there, and she let me hold her hand when the pains came. I was grateful for that because I was scared. Like I said, Mrs. Dobbs could be kind sometimes. Sure, I'd seen other women in labor because Mrs. Dobbs often went to help out when a baby was coming, and she'd have me go with her. All I can say is that seeing somebody else in labor and going through it yourself are not the same. It's a whole lot scarier when it's you.

Finally, the doctor came, and he must have brought some chloroform because there's part of it that I don't remember. I remember some of it, though, like the doctor saying it would probably be a while before the baby came because first babies take longer. For just a little while at least, that gave me something to think about besides the pain. I thought about *first* babies. That made me think maybe one day I'd have a second baby if I could get a husband first.

Before long, though, I was telling myself I was never going to have another baby because it hurt too much, and I was cussing Clarence in my mind for getting me into this. I just wished it was *him* who was hurting like this. The last part hurt terrible bad, and I screamed real loud. Then I felt her come out of me.

"It's a girl," the doctor said, and I said, "Annabelle."

I thought he would put her on my stomach after he swatted her and made her cry, but he didn't. Instead, he wrapped her in the blanket and gave her to Mrs. Dobbs. She walked out of the room with her, cooing to her like it was her own baby. I don't remember pushing the afterbirth out. I guess I was too upset to remember. I do recall telling the doctor that I wanted to see my baby.

"You will," he said, "in due time."

Due time, I learned, is a really long time. Several hours. I tried to sleep, but I couldn't. Finally, Mrs. Dobbs brought Annabelle in and helped me get started nursing her. That was the best thing that had ever happened to me. Nursing my baby made me feel so close to her. Like we were connected to each other and belonged to each other. I loved looking at her while she nursed. I stroked her fine blond hair and touched the silky skin on her cheek that was wrinkled like a little old lady.

Mrs. Dobbs was nice to me. She brought me my meals for the first two days and brought Annabelle to me to nurse. Every minute with her was precious to me, even changing her messy diapers. By the third day, I was up and around, not only taking care of

Annabelle but also helping out in the kitchen some. It was the end of the second week when the people from the Red Cross and the welfare office came.

I guess both Mr. and Mrs. Dobbs must have known they were coming because Mr. Dobbs came home for lunch that day and never went back to work. I thought at first that maybe he was feeling poorly, but I didn't ask, of course. It sure never occurred to me what was really going on, that is not until I saw that Red Cross on the nurse's hat. Then I knew it couldn't be anything good. It had been easy for me to put it all out of my mind until now, since I spent every free minute I had with Annabelle. Maybe I was just too tired to think about it because Annabelle woke me up so many times every night. I wasn't getting more than three or four hours of sleep. I didn't mind even that because I had never loved anyone so much in my whole life as I loved my baby.

I don't know what the Red Cross people said because I stayed out of the room with my daughter. When they left and nothing changed for me, I started to think everything was going to be all right after all. Then, on the day that Annabelle was five weeks old, Mr. and Mrs. Dobbs called me into the living room after I finished the supper dishes. I wasn't expecting anything, and all I could think was that I didn't want to stay up and talk because I was so tired, and since Annabelle was asleep, I might be able to steal a few hours of sleep before she woke up again.

"Sit down and let's talk," Mr. Dobbs said, motioning toward the sofa. They almost never invited me to sit down with them and talk, but even then I wasn't worried. All I could think about was sleep.

Mr. Dobbs cleared his throat and moved around in his chair, settling himself. "Carrie, I'm sure you remember the hearing in front of Judge Shackelford, don't you?"

"Yes sir." I didn't add that I wished I could forget about it.

"Well, the time has come for you to go."

I felt like the wind had been knocked out of me. "But what about my baby?" I said. "I got to be here to take care of her."

"Now don't you worry about Vivian," Mrs. Dobbs said. "We're

gonna take care of her. We worked it out with the welfare people, and they're even going to give us a little money to help out. She'll be took care of just like you was."

I couldn't speak, and I felt as if I was going to lose my supper right there in front of them. She had called her Vivian. She *knew* her name was Annabelle, and it gave me no comfort whatsoever to think of her being brought up in their house the way I was.

"You'll be leaving on the train next week," Mr. Dobbs said. "I think you'll like it there. You'll be took care of, and you'll be with your mama."

"Vivian will be six weeks old by the time you leave, so you've had a good bit of time with her, and it's time you go on and do what's best for her and you and all of us," Mrs. Dobbs said.

I still couldn't speak at first. It was like all of my words had been sucked out of me, along with my soul, until finally I managed four words.

"Her name is Annabelle."

It was an unusually hot day for May, the kind of day that always reminded me of sticky fingers touching me from my head to my toes. That's the way I felt as I left the Dobbses' house to get on the train to Lynchburg, where I would be met and taken to Madison Heights.

I didn't sleep at all the night before we were to leave because it was my last night with Annabelle. I held her in my arm all night long and let her nurse when she wanted to. Mrs. Dobbs had been trying for a while to get me to wean her to a bottle, and now I knew why. She wanted her weaned by the time I left. Annabelle didn't take to the bottle very well though. She would just spit the rubber nipple out and cry. That made me worry that she wouldn't eat at all after I left. All I could do was hope that Mrs. Dobbs wouldn't let her starve to death.

It must have been around four thirty or five o'clock in the morning when Mrs. Dobbs came into my room and saw me sitting up in bed with Annabelle at my breast. I thought she would be mad and have a fit when she saw it, but she didn't. I wouldn't have cared if she did, to tell the truth. All I could feel was sadness.

She came over to the bed and took hold of Annabelle, pulling her little mouth away from my nipple. Annabelle didn't even wake up. She just kept working her mouth like she was still sucking.

"It's time for me to take her now," Mrs. Dobbs said. "You better try to get some sleep. You got a big day ahead of you."

"I don't want to sleep!" I said. "Let me have her back. I. . ."

She paid me no mind, closing the door behind her as she left the room with my baby. I jumped out of bed and ran after her. I made it to the door of the bedroom she shared with Mr. Dobbs just as she closed it, and I heard the lock click. I banged on the door as hard as I could and cried out for her to give Annabelle back to me.

"Go back to bed, Carrie. You'll wake up Vivian." Just as Mrs. Dobbs said that, I heard Annabelle whimper and then cry the way she did when she was disturbed. I felt that warm tingle of milk surging in my breasts like it always did at the sound of her cry, but all I could do was let my own tears fall as I turned around and went back to my room. I didn't want to upset Annabelle even more.

Of course I didn't sleep at all, but I got out of bed at my usual time and was dressed by six o'clock. I went to the kitchen just like I always did, but instead of firing up the stove to cook breakfast, I found myself a cold biscuit and a little bit of milk. I couldn't eat a bite of it though. All I could do was listen for the sweet sound of Annabelle's morning cry while I sat at the table in the kitchen.

There was nothing but silence for what seemed like forever. Finally, I heard her, and I sprang to my feet. It was such a familiar sound to me now, so much a part of me that I didn't know how I was going to be able to live without it. I went to the Dobbses' bedroom door and knocked.

"She's all right, Carrie. Go on about your business," Mrs. Dobbs called from behind the locked door. I didn't move. I just stood there, and I could hear her cooing and talking baby talk to Annabelle, calling her Little Vivian. I was still standing there after what must have been at least half an hour when Mrs. Dobbs opened the door. She was holding Annabelle. She looked at me, not saying a word, and walked toward the kitchen. I followed, watching Annabelle's face. She had lost the newborn wrinkles; her cheeks were all chubby softness, and her wide, bright eyes were trying to focus.

"Well, where's the coffee?" Mrs. Dobbs said as she walked into the kitchen. "Oh," she said, catching herself, "I guess you didn't have to--"

"I'll take Annabelle," I said, reaching for her.

"No, I don't think you should do..."

Before she could finish her sentence, I had Annabelle in my arms.

"You better burp her," Mrs. Dobbs said. "I just gave her a bottle."

All I could do was stare at her, hating her for doing it.

"She took it just fine," Mrs. Dobbs said.

I put Annabelle to my shoulder, patting her gently on the back to make any air bubbles she might have swallowed come up. As I walked away from the kitchen, I met Mr. Dobbs as he came through the living room on his way to the kitchen.

"We'll be leaving in about fifteen minutes," he said. "You don't want to be late for the train."

"Don't I?" I said, but I said it too quiet for Mr. Dobbs to hear. He was on his way out the door to the outhouse and probably wouldn't have heard me even if I'd said it louder.

I sat down on the sofa, holding Annabelle on my lap so I could see her face. She seemed to be looking back at me, and her lips moved, just a little. It was like she was smiling. Or maybe it was just baby twitches. Whatever it was, it was precious to me. Her lips were such a pretty dark pink and her skin pale with fine blue veins showing through. I could look at her forever. I wouldn't think about leaving her. I wouldn't cry. She would know it if I cried. She would know it if I felt sad.

It could not have been fifteen minutes before Mr. Dobbs came into the living room and told me to get my things because it was time to go. He must have come back inside without me hearing the door, and he must have taken the time to eat because he was wiping his mouth with the palm of his hand, telling me again to get my things. I didn't move, except to pull Annabelle closer to me, with her head cradled in the crook of my arm so I could see her face. She closed her eyes and moved her mouth like she was nursing, and then she grimaced just a little like she was dreaming. Would she ever dream of me? Would she even remember me?

Someone, Mr. Dobbs maybe, must have gone to my room to fetch the suitcase I'd packed with the few things I owned because it was sitting at my feet now, and Mrs. Dobbs had hold of my arm, pulling me to my feet.

"You go on now, Carrie. This is what's best for you." She reached for Annabelle, but I pulled her even closer to me—up to my face so I could kiss her velvety cheek, nuzzle the dampness of her neck under her chin and smell the sweetness that belonged to her alone. Then she was gone from my arms. They ached with emptiness.

22

CARRIE

The Red Cross nurse handed me over to another nurse when we got to Lynchburg, and we drove out to the Colony in Madison Heights. I never learned the new nurse's name, and all she said to me was "Get in" when we got to her car. She spoke not another word until she stopped the car in front of a two-story brick building with steps leading up to a wide porch and double doors. Other two-story brick buildings that looked more or less the same were close by, reminding me of a cluster of rotting brick-red grapes. The grass was pretty at least. It looked like a carpet and was the greenest I've ever seen. Big trees had already leafed out, and the way the breeze ruffled them made me think of beautiful women showing off their spring dresses.

The nurse went with me into an office where a woman pecking on a typewriter told us we had to wait until Dr. Priddy was ready to see me. It occurred to me that I'd been doing a lot of that lately—waiting in offices for some man to come out and tell me what direction my life was going to take.

This waiting room was different from the one in the courthouse though. The floor wasn't polished, and there were no rugs on the floor or pictures on the wall. The paint on the walls was peeling in places. There was a smell in the room, too, like lye soap mixed with alcohol. I thought for a minute it was going to make me sick. I was nervous because I didn't know what this Dr. Priddy was going to make me do.

Finally, the typewriter lady took me in to see Dr. Priddy, and the nurse went with me. He was sitting there at his desk—round face, big ears, and light-brown hair parted in the middle. I would say he was ordinary looking except for the grayish look of his skin. He looked up when I entered his office with the nurse behind me.

"This is Carrie Buck?"

"Yes, Doctor," the nurse said.

He glanced at the papers in front of him. "Everything is in order, it seems." Then, looking up at me again, he said, "You have been classified as a high-grade moron and highly morally deficient. You'll be staying with us here at the Colony, Carrie. I think you'll like it here."

What made him think I would like it here? I didn't like the idea of being locked up in any kind of place, no matter how pretty the grass and trees were. And why did he call me a moron? I'd heard that word before, and it was an insult for him to call me that.

"You have your belongings with you, I see." Dr. Priddy was eyeing my suitcase.

I nodded my head and tried to say "yes sir," but I was too nervous for it to come out.

"Very good," he said. "Wilson, show her to second ward in Drewry-Gillian."

"Yes, Doctor," the nurse said. She took my arm and, without a word to me, led me out of the office and out of the building.

I was a little confused. This Dr. Priddy sure wasn't the kind of doctor I was used to. He didn't ask me any questions about how I felt, and he didn't wear one of those things around his neck that they use to listen to people's hearts. I'd never seen a doctor before who just sat behind a desk and told people where to go.

We'd walked maybe a couple of blocks until we came to another red-brick building with a sign in the front that said Drewry-Gillian Building. The nurse hadn't said a word to me during the entire walk. At least I knew her name was Wilson because that's what Dr. Priddy had called her. Once we were inside the building, I noticed that it had the same smell as Dr. Priddy's building. Kind of sickening. The nurse led me upstairs to a room lined with beds. A few women and girls were sitting on the beds, reading or talking to each other.

"This will be your bed," Wilson said, leading me up to a single bed so narrow I wasn't sure I'd fit on it, especially since I hadn't lost all the weight I'd gained when I was pregnant. "Unpack your things and put them in the chest next to your bed. Store your suitcase under the bed. The toilets, sinks, and showers are there," she said, pointing to a door a few yards away from my bed. "You'll be told when you can go to the dining room for lunch, and you'll be given your work assignment tomorrow." With that, she started to walk to the door.

"When can I see my mama?" My voice sounded weak and shaky as I called out to her back. I wasn't sure if I was supposed to say anything.

Wilson turned around to look at me. "No doubt you'll see her at lunch. She's at her work assignment now."

"Oh," I said. After a bit, I managed to say, "Thank you," but she was already out the door.

Just about the time I finished unpacking my suitcase, I heard a bell ring. It was the same kind of bell they used at my school. It made me sad at first, made me remember once again how much I'd wanted to go back to school. The handful of girls and women who were in the room got up from their beds and went to the door.

"Time to eat," one of them called over her shoulder to me. "Follow me."

I followed. We went downstairs to another big room, this one lined with tables and smelling of onions. Everybody was sitting down at the tables. I didn't know what to do, didn't know where I was supposed to sit. I felt like crying. I guess I would have embarrassed myself by bawling like a baby right then and there if I hadn't spotted Mama. She was coming into the dining room with two other women.

"Mama!" I called, walking to her. As soon as the word was out of my mouth, I was embarrassed because some of the people around the table I was closest to were looking at me.

Mama looked up with a surprised expression on her face. "Carrie? That you? What you doing here?"

"They put me in the Colony." By this time I was close enough to her that I didn't have to shout.

"What.?"

"Said I'm feebleminded. But that's not the real reason. It's 'cause I had a baby."

Mama laughed. That surprised me. I didn't see anything to laugh about. "Damn," she said, "if that don't beat all." She took my arm and led me to a table. "Come on and sit down. The food here ain't half bad."

Women in white aprons were bringing trays with tin bowls full of what looked like stew, along with tin cups full of milk. Big chunks of cornbread were resting in baskets on the tables. Almost as soon as I sat down, one of the bowls of stew was in front of me. Mama was already eating hers before I could pick up my spoon. I tasted mine, and it was good, just like Mama said. The cornbread wasn't bad, but I would have added a little baking powder and maybe another egg. Mama was enjoying every bite. She'd obviously enjoyed several meals because she'd gained weight. Her color was better than the last time I saw her, and she looked clean, even her hair. It was good to know she was at least being taken care of.

Mama filled her mouth with cornbread and washed it down with some milk. "I'm working in the sewing department," she said, still chewing. "Ain't bad. Everybody has to work, and sewing's one of the best jobs. Don't have to be out in the weather, and you get to sit. I'll see if I can't get you in there, too."

"Thank you," I said, "but I don't know how to sew."

She shrugged and stuffed even more cornbread in her mouth. "Hell, you think I did? They teach you." She picked up her bowl, and I could hear her teeth clinking against the tin rim as she slurped the last of the stew. "I'll tell you something," she said after she'd drained the bowl. "I ain't never been cold at night since I been here. Got my own bed with sheets on it. Plenty of blankets, too, if you need 'em, and they give me some clothes. Give me this dress and another one for when this one's dirty. Comin' here's the best thing that's happened to me. Ain't bad at all. Get plenty of rest. Ain't no men around to bother you. Some of the women that's here complains about not being able to get out, go to town, stuff like that. Not me. I had all of that I want. Ain't nothin' in town I can't get right here." She poked a finger at the table as she spoke that last sentence. "Well, there ain't no booze here, but what the hell. Doin' without is better than bein' cold. Would help if I had a little money to buy stuff like another dress and some soap to wash it in. They don't give you everything, I guess, but I ain't complainin'."

She went on talking about what it was like at the Colony—how she could listen to the radio while she sewed, how she enjoyed gossiping and joking with her fellow workers, and on and on until the bell rang again. Then she went back to work, and I went back to my room. She hadn't asked me a single question about my baby—where she was now, what her name was. She hadn't asked about Roy and Doris or anything at all about me or the world outside of the Colony.

When I got back to my ward, there was a woman waiting for me. She said she was there to give me orientation. I didn't know what that was, but it wasn't anything scary. She just told me all the rules about where I was supposed to be at certain times, and she said I would be working in the kitchen.

"First you must be examined by the doctor, however," she said. "It's routine for all inmates, but if you're going to be working in the kitchen, we want to make sure you're disease free." Somehow she managed to make me feel dirty just by standing there and looking at me.

She took me to yet another one of those big, old brick buildings, and as soon as I walked in, I knew it was a hospital. It had that smell. She told me to sit while she went to talk to a nurse. I heard her give the nurse my name and say I was there for the entry exam. After that, she told me to stay where I was until I was called, and then she left.

I wished I'd had something to do while I waited because it was a long wait. There weren't any books or magazines around like I saw in the doctor's office back in Charlottesville the time I was there. I tried to doze, but I couldn't fall asleep because I was too nervous. Mostly, though, I just tried not to think because, if I did, it made me sad, and I didn't want to start crying.

When I finally got to see the doctor, I could see that he was more the kind of doctor I was used to than Dr. Priddy had been. This one had a white coat and that thing to listen to hearts flung around his neck. A nurse had already made me change into a gown before the doctor came in.

"Carrie Buck?" he said when he saw me.

I was about to tell him that yes, I was Carrie Buck, but the nurse answered for me. She called him Dr. Bell. He went to a sink, washed his hands, and came toward me. He tilted my head back, holding on to my chin, and started talking to the nurse while she wrote down whatever he was saying.

"Low, narrow forehead; high cheekbones; dark complected white woman." He made me stand up and then added, "Slight build." He listened to my heart and looked in my ears, and then he made me lie down while he prodded my belly and looked at my privates. All the time he was telling the nurse what he saw. "Glandular condition of the stomach indicates she's recently had a child," he said. He could have just asked, and I would have told him that. Finally he said, "Good general health, clean body, free from eruptions, well nourished."

After that, he went over to a sink, washed his hands again, and left the room. I was told to go back to my ward. By the time I got there, it was time to leave again to go to the dining room for supper. Mama was there, and she was just as talkative as she was at noon. I couldn't tell you what she said though. I just couldn't keep my mind on things.

After supper, Mama wanted to show me her ward. That surprised me. She had never made any effort to invite me anywhere or to be with me before. It turned out her ward looked just like mine, and it was crowded with just as many beds.

"Come on," she said, beckoning with her finger. "I'll show you the porch. We can sit out there a little while." She led me to the side of the room that faced the front and went out onto a big veranda. "See," she said, "it's got screen all around it so the mosquitoes won't bother you." She had a big grin on her face, as if she was showing off her own fancy house.

We found two rocking chairs side by side, and we each sat in one. It felt kind of muggy sitting on that porch, but there was a smell of fresh-cut grass in the air that was nice.

Mama sat beside me rocking contentedly, and she had finally stopped talking. I tried to be happy, or at least satisfied, but I just couldn't. All I could do was think about Annabelle. I could tell when it was time for her to nurse because my milk hadn't dried up completely, and I would leak a little when it was time for her to eat. I wondered how she was doing with the bottle, if she missed me as much as I missed her, and if Mrs. Dobbs was taking good care of her. I felt Mama's eyes on me and knew that she was looking at me and could see the tears I couldn't hold back streaming down my face.

"Now there ain't no need to cry, Carrie. Worse things could happen to you, and you'll get used to being here."

"No I won't. I'll never get used to being without Annabelle." I wiped at my tears with the backs of my hands.

"Who's Annabelle?"

"That's my daughter. They took her away from me."

"Good Lord, Carrie, there ain't nothing you can do about that."

"Well, I know that." I wiped away more tears and sniffed because my nose was running.

"Here," Mama said and handed me a handkerchief. "Now hush." She was silent for a long time. "You get used to it," she said again.

"I don't want to get used to it."

"Well, you got to."

The sharp way she spoke made me turn and look at her. She was staring straight ahead, and her mouth had turned into a hard, thin line. Was she thinking about having to give up her own babies? First me, then Roy and Doris? I didn't want to ask her that. It would make me sad whether she said yes or no, so I just turned my eyes from her and stared ahead at nothing just like she was doing.

Biennial Report to the State of Virginia
For the Virginia State Colony for the Feebleminded and Epileptic
(Excerpts)
By
Dr. Albert Priddy, Superintendent

Each day that I work in the custodial care of delinquent, high-grade moron girls and women of good physical strength and health impresses me with the gravity of the responsibility which the management of institutions for the feebleminded assume in keeping these people indefinitely to restrain them from overt acts of immorality. If they are to be kept from indulging in sexual immorality, it means they are to be kept a lifetime in institutions under the strictest custody. Besides the inhumane aspect of this, a large percent of the girls and women of this class should be earning their own living in work for which they are mentally and physically adequate, rather than to constitute lifetime burdens on taxpayers of the State. It certainly seems more humane and just to them to give them the benefit of a milder and less severe method of attaining the desired end of preventing sexual immorality. Therefore, every reasonable and fair-minded person must concede that the the withdrawal of the right to propagate their kind could and should be given to society in such cases of females as have demonstrated their constitutional mental and moral inability to use the right of child-bearing as a blessing to humanity rather than a curse.

The admission of female morons to this institution has consisted for the most part of those who would formerly have found their way into the red-light district and become dangerous to society. These women are never reformed in heart and mind because they are defectives from the standpoint of intellect and moral conception. I view sterilization of mental defectives as the only solution to the problem of the custodial care of them by the state.

The superintendents of the four State hospitals and the Colony

152

have been appointed to a committee by the General State Hospital Board to draft a bill to be presented in the coming General Assembly for a law authorizing the sterilization of such patients as may be found capable of earning their own living and of being released under proper custodial care, without danger to themselves and the public. It is to be to be hoped that with the best legal talent to draft such a bill, it can come within constitutional limits and enacted into law.

23

LOUISA

ouisa had just finished a solitary dinner in the Manhattan apartment her parents owned and found herself with nothing to do. She'd decided to come to New York to research some documents she needed for her project on deviant women and stole a few hours to spend the night in the apartment her parents kept in the city.

Her parents were busy with their own lives, so her visit with them so far had been brief. Her father had left early in the afternoon for Washington to attend meetings that had to do with a world economic conference scheduled for some time next year in Geneva. Her mother was attending one of her board meetings. The opera board, Louisa thought. Or maybe it was the museum or an art gallery.

She wandered into the library, looking for something to read. There were shelves lined with the classics, texts on economic policy and history, and even several current novels. She pulled the new Agatha Christie novel, *The Murder on the Links,* from a shelf and opened it. She read two entire pages without knowing what she'd read. For some reason, she couldn't concentrate.

Her thoughts whirled, making her feel as if a storm was raging in her head. Lemuel's last letter had been unsettling. Why should he be so critical of her work? Shouldn't he be as supportive of her as she was of him? Why hadn't she heard from him again? When she'd broached the subject with her mother, she laughed and told her not to be so naive. She failed to see how she was being naive, but her mother wouldn't discuss it further. Besides Lemuel's letter, there was also her research. It had proven to be exhausting, and there was so much still to do, so many things to learn. She'd been excited about her interview with Carrie Buck at the courthouse in Charlottesville, but she needed more interviews like that. She also needed more time with Carrie, more time to examine the link between a mother and daughter who were both mental and moral deviants.

Sliding the book back to its assigned space on the shelf, she turned away, thinking she might try listening to the radio. As she walked toward the large console with its dials, centered needle, and fabric-covered speakers, she spied the *Times* folded on one of the tables. She picked it up, thinking she might find a story by Ben Newman, but his byline wasn't on the front page. When she opened the paper to the second page, she saw the phone number for the editorial offices. Ben had told her he often worked late into the night. Would he be there now?

She reached for the telephone on the same table that held the paper, not allowing herself to consider that she was about to do something she shouldn't do, and picked up the receiver from its cradle. When the operator asked for the number, she gave it to her and waited. Her chest felt tight, and she knew her heart was beating too fast. She was about to hang up when another voice told her she'd reached the *New York Times* and asked for the party she was trying to reach.

"Ben Newman, please." Her voice sounded odd as if it belonged to someone else. He wouldn't be there, of course. It was foolish of her to think he would be. The thought calmed her. In the next moment, she heard his voice.

"Ben Newman here."

"Hello, Ben." There was nothing else to say, was there? Her chest tightened again.

"Who is this?"

"I'm sorry," she said. "I shouldn't have—"

"Louisa? Is that you?"

"Yes, it's Louisa." Her voice sounded breathy and unsteady.

"I thought I recognized your voice. Where are you?"

"I'm here. In Manhattan."

"Can I see you?"

"Well..."

"Listen," he said before she could say more, "call a cab and meet me at the Cyprus. It's on Broadway near Times Square."

"I, well, all right. The Cyprus."

Her voice shook when she called for a taxi. "What am I doing?" she asked herself aloud when she hung up the phone. Calling a friend, that's all, she told herself. A friend who was knowledgeable about the eugenics movement. This would be a chance to get more of his perspective than she'd been able to get the last time she spoke with him.

She had managed to calm herself considerably by the time the cab driver wound through the busy streets, stopped in front of the Cyprus, and opened the door for her. She paid him and hurried inside.

The Cyprus was not the kind of place she usually frequented when she was in New York, but it was a decent restaurant, decent enough to have a maître d'. When she gave him her name, he nodded, asked her to follow him, and showed her to the booth where Ben was waiting.

Ben stood as soon as he saw her. "Louisa!" He took her hand and brought it to his lips. "How wonderful to see you!" He helped her sit and settled in across from her.

"I hope I didn't take you away from something important," she said.

"Nonsense," he said. "Have you had dinner?"

"Yes." She was feeling nervous again, wishing for one of the cigarettes her friend and roommate Flora had recently introduced her to.

"So have I," Ben said. "We'll have an appetizer." He summoned a waiter and ordered shrimp cocktails. "What brings you to New York? Besides Mama and Papa, I mean."

"I'm here to search for some documents in the public library," she said. "I hope to be able to find some records of studies done on a family upstate with several feebleminded members."

"For your book," he said.

"Yes," she answered and returned the smile he'd given her.

"How's the book progressing?" he asked.

"Slowly, I'm afraid. I've made some progress, however. I was able to interview a young feebleminded woman named Carrie Buck, whom I believe is going to provide me with insight if I can manage to see her again. There's so much to learn."

"I'm sure there is."

She frowned at a nuance she thought she heard in his voice. "You still don't approve of my work," she said.

He frowned. "That's not the case at all. I have a feeling it's going to be important."

"But you don't agree with my premise."

"That sterilization is the answer to the ills of society? No, I don't agree, but that's no reason for you to stop your research. Mind if I smoke?" he asked and reached inside a pocket for a pack of cigarettes.

"No. Do you mind if I do? "

He smiled, offered her a cigarette, and lit it for her.

"I have no intention of stopping my research, by the way," she said, blowing out the smoke.

"Good. I hope you find some answers."

"Like who gets to decide who is deviant and who isn't?"

"Yes," he said. "That and other things."

"Such as?"

"Such as how do you measure normality? How do you account for differences in culture, religion, and upbringing? Do we all have to conform to some outsider's idea of morality? Or even intellect? Have you considered that some are denied education?"

"Of course, I've considered that, and—"

"And race? People like me? Does that come into play when deciding who is and isn't deviant?"

Louisa was startled by his question. "Why would you ask such a question? You're not Negro."

"I'm Jewish."

"I can assure you there are many Jewish people active in our movement. I can also assure you that I have and continue to consider all of those points you made."

"Good."

"I'm not looking for your approval," she said with more anger in her voice than she intended. "I'm well aware that different cultures may have moral standards different from ours. The point is moral deviancy is measured by culture."

"Is it indeed? How about Mrs. Sanger?"

"You're referring to her ideas concerning her liaisons."

"I'm referring to the fact that she sleeps with men other than her husband."

"She's a highly intelligent woman. Those of her cerebral capacity often experiment in various ways."

Ben's smile reappeared. "I see, and do you consider yourself intelligent and of a cerebral bent?"

"I..." Louisa suddenly felt tongue-tied, and she knew she was blushing.

"Forgive me for asking," Ben said. "I didn't mean to upset you." He smiled. "Well, maybe I did, but let's talk about something else."

"Ben, it's important that you understand that I'm not an elitist and that I'm open to considering all sides of the question."

"I hope so," he said. "By the way, have you ever been to a speakeasy?"

"Uh..." Louisa knew about speakeasies, but she hesitated to admit that she'd never been to one. It would only confirm Ben's idea of her naiveté.

"A nightclub."

"Well, I didn't come of age until after Prohibition was enacted, so—"

"You would be of age now, I assume."

"Of course, but—"

"Come on," he said. "Let's go." He stood, laid a bill on the table, and helped her up.

Louisa glanced at the bill. It was ten dollars—a lot of money for someone like Ben and more than enough to pay the check and a tip. She hesitated a moment, thinking she would offer to pay, but she let it pass and let him guide her out of the restaurant.

He hailed a taxi and gave the driver directions to an address on Bedford Street in Greenwich. When the taxi stopped in front of a small three-story building squeezed between two other buildings, Ben helped her out and escorted her to a nondescript door.

"Welcome to Chumley's," he said. He knocked on the door with three staccato taps, followed by a pause and two more taps.

Louisa had heard some of her friends at school talk of Chumley's, and she had built a picture in her mind of something quite different—something not so uninteresting in its appearance. There was not even a sign in front to inform participants. There was only a plain-faced building and a cheap wooden door.

The door opened, but only slightly. Louisa could see a pair of eyes peering through the small opening. Ben said something, one word spoken in a low voice she couldn't understand, and the door opened wider. Ben ushered her into a noisy, smoky room full of tables where men and women were seated. All of them seemed to be laughing, and all of them seemed to be drinking from cocktail glasses. The dance floor was crowded with couples clinging to each other while a small band with a single cornet played "Everybody Loves My Baby." The cornet player moved his instrument from his lips long enough to sing in a gravely voice.

"Do you recognize him?" Ben asked.

Louisa stared at the man with his broad, toothy smile. "Is that—?"

"Louie Armstrong," Ben said. "Come on, let's dance." He pulled her onto the floor and held her away from him enough to allow her to move with freedom to the sultry jazz as Armstrong switched to a trumpet for "West End Blues."

When the song ended, he led her to a table and ordered two gin and tonics.

"Oh, I don't think I should," she said. "I'm so unaccustomed to drinking alcohol. Only a little wine now and then when Mother feels adventurous enough to serve it, and I've never had gin."

"Never had gin? Too bad."

She answered with a shrug that made him laugh.

Louisa looked around at the room full of people. There were tables and a dance floor but no bar. Drinks appeared on waiter's trays from some hidden room. The walls were lined with pictures of people, most of whom she didn't know, but she recognized one of them.

"Look, isn't that John Reed's picture?" she asked.

"The one and only," Ben said. "Father of the Communist Party of America. They say he used to come in here all the time. See the fellow in the corner over there? Recognize him?"

Louisa looked at the man with a long, thin face decorated with a perfectly groomed triangular mustache. He alternately sipped a cocktail and spoke with animation to a man and woman at the table with him.

"Eugene O'Neill," Ben said. "Ever hear of him?"

"Oh!" Louisa was momentarily starstruck. Of course she'd heard of him. Everyone had, and everyone knew about his edgy plays—the one about a racially mixed marriage and an abusive white wife in particular. She'd never seen it, but her parents considered it scandalous. She'd vowed to see another of his plays which was experiencing a revival and was all the talk of the campus.

"*Emperor Jones*," she said. "It's supposed to be about a black man who flees to a foreign country and declares himself emperor."

"It's experiencing a revival," Ben said.

"Yes, I know."

"Would you like to see it? I think I can get tickets. They often provide a few extras to the *Times*."

"I..." She hesitated. "That's a generous offer, but—"

"But what? You can't go because you're engaged to be married? Don't worry. I won't steal you away from him."

"Still, I—"

"Here are our drinks," he said before she could finish her protest. He lifted one of the glasses and handed it to her. "Try it."

She did. It burned slightly but felt oddly smooth as it slid down her throat. Within a few minutes, they were joined at their table by a man named Oliver Anderson, a fellow journalist at the *Times*, and his girlfriend who said her name was Pearl. She had scandalous blond hair and painted nails.

"Pleased to meetcha," Pearl said and giggled, obviously tipsy, when she was introduced to Louisa. She turned to Oliver then and said, "Order me another, will ya please, Ollie?"

Louisa took another sip of her drink and listened while Oliver and Ben talked about Germany and the League of Nations. Pearl tried to engage her in a conversation about something her hairdresser had told her about called a "permanent wave."

"Makes your hair curly, just like you were born that way. Can't wait to get one," Pearl said, slurring her words. She segued into talk of Clara Bow. "She's the It girl," she said, "and I'm sure even college girls like you know what *it* means, 'specially if you've ever done *it*." She giggled again and began describing her favorite movie, *Daughters of Pleasure*, while Louisa sipped at her second drink which had somehow appeared in front of her. "It's one of Clara's early ones, before the talkies," Pearl said, "but she plays this really naughty French girl who is sleeping with her best friend's daddy. Talk about juicy! I would love to—Oh, they're playing the 'Charleston,' Ollie. Let's dance!" She took Ollie's hand and pulled him onto the dance floor.

"Sorry about that," Ben said when they left the table. "I kept trying to rescue you from her, but I didn't seem to be able to—"

"Oh, never mind," Louisa said with a wave of her hand. She was surprised to hear herself giggle. "I found her amusing, actually. Do you know what an It girl is?"

"I think I do," Ben said as he helped her up and led her to the dance floor. "Come on, Louie, they're playing our song."

"Louie?" No one had ever called her that before, and the sound of it made her laugh.

She had danced to "Charleston" many times with the girls in the dorm but never on a public dance floor. "Not bad!" Ben exclaimed as he stood back and let her dance. She was soon joined by a line of other girls who linked arms with her to kick their legs and move their knees rhythmically with their palms on their kneecaps. The dance ended with all of them laughing and Louisa falling against Ben. She was still laughing when the band began "Rhapsody in Blue," and Ben pulled her to him. They swayed together, holding each other closely. She felt sleepy and laid her head on his shoulder. She felt him kiss her hair, but she didn't move her head until the music ended. When she started to pull away, he kissed her firmly on the lips. Once again, she didn't move away.

He kissed her one more time, lightly on the lips, when the taxi he had called pulled up in front of her parents' house, and he walked her to the door.

"Good night, Louie," he whispered.

To: Louisa Van Patten, Bryn Mawr College
From: Ben Newman, New York Times
September 23, 1924

Dear Louisa,

I thought you would want to know about developments in the question of deviant women and eugenics in Virginia. I've gained some information from a confidential source that will likely be of interest to you.

If you are able to meet me at the Cypress in New York on the 30th, I will be happy to give you the information.

Cordially,
Ben

To: Dr. Albert Priddy, Superintendent, Virginia State Colony for Epileptics and Feebleminded, Madison Heights, Virginia
From: Caroline Wilhelm, Red Cross Superintendent of Public Welfare, Albemarle County, Charlottesville, Virginia
October 2, 1924

My dear Dr. Priddy,

    I do not recall and am unable to find any mention in our files of having said that Carrie Buck's baby was mentally defected. In a previous letter, I said that we should not want to take the responsibility of placing so young a child whose mother and grandmother are both mental defectives.

Caroline Wilhelm

24

LOUISA

"You had dinner with a friend. So what?" Flora, Louisa's roommate, said after Louisa confided in her.

"But if Lemuel should ever do such—"

Flora laughed with a snort. "You're not married to Lemuel yet. Enjoy life while you can. Believe me, the fun will end once you hook yourself up with that stuffed shirt."

"Lemuel's not a stuffed shirt, Flora, not really. You just don't know him very well."

"Do you?" Flora gave her an accusing look.

"Of course I do! What are you getting at?"

Flora answered with a shrug,. "Nothing, I guess. It's your life."

Louisa tried to soothe her conscience by telling herself that Flora was right—she wasn't married to anyone yet. Anyway, it had all been completely innocent. A few glasses of gin and a dance or two meant nothing. The kisses? Well, that just happened, but it would never happen again because she'd vowed never to see Ben again.

She'd seen his return address on the envelope when she picked up her mail. She felt her heartbeat quicken and ripped it open immediately. It only took a few seconds to read the note. He was asking her to contact him again the next time she was in the city. "I have information pertinent to your book I would like to discuss with you," the note said. It was signed, "Cordially, Ben."

Louisa had given the note a careless fling, letting it land among the mound of papers on her desk. The note was curt, almost formal—at least businesslike. For a moment she felt offended. But why would it be anything other than a short, businesslike note? She was sure Ben had not given their evening together at the speakeasy another thought—not the laughter, not the dancing, not the way it had felt when their bodies were so close together, and certainly not the kisses.

She'd had no idea when she would be in the city again, and if she did go, there would probably be precious little time to contact him.

Yet, by the end of the week, she'd made a plan to go. After all, the New York Public Library was a treasure trove of information—information she needed as research for her book. It was relatively easy to get there, and why not contact a friend for lunch while she was there?

A week later Louisa watched fine, sparse drops of rain discolor the sidewalk on Broadway near Times Square while she sat near the window of the Cypress where Ben had said he would meet her. A waiter had brought her a complimentary glass of ginger ale, but she'd hardly touched it. She was nervous about seeing Ben.

She saw him across the street, shoulders hunched and hat pulled down over his face against the scant, intermittent rain. She sat up a little straighter, and her breath came a little quicker. Another long draw on the cigarette would calm her nerves. He entered the restaurant, brushing rain from his sleeves and handing his hat to the maître d'. Looking around, he found her quickly, as if he'd felt her eyes upon him. Smiling, he spoke briefly to the maître d' and hurried toward her.

"You are devastatingly glamorous with that cigarette and that cloche hat, not to mention those eyes."

She stubbed out her cigarette. "You're very flattering."

"Not at all. I meant it." He accepted a menu from a waiter. "Have you ordered?"

"No, I was waiting for you."

He looked at her from over the top of the menu. "Hmmm," he said.

She wondered what he meant. "What is this information you have for me?"

"Well, aren't you in a hurry?" His tone sounded more teasing than sarcastic, and he was smiling in his usual charming manner.

"I'm sorry, but I suppose I *am* in a bit of a hurry. I have a lot of writing to do. I can do some of it on the train going back, of course, but then I'm sure I'll still be up until quite—"

"Why are you so nervous, Louie?"

He caught her off guard by calling her Louie, the name he'd given her the last time they were together. She liked the casual, intimate sound of it. "I...I don't know why you think I'm nervous. I'm not, of course, just a bit rushed because—"

"I make you nervous."

"That's ridiculous. Why would I be nervous around anyone when we're only having lunch?"

"Why are you pretending?"

"Pretending?" She was making a show of studying the menu.

"Pretending that nothing happened last time, Louie."

She closed the menu and put it aside. "We went to a nightclub together. We both got a little drunk. We had a good time—in my case, maybe a better time than I should have. That's all that happened."

"You had a better time than you should have? What's that supposed to mean?"

"You know what it means. I am in love with a good, decent man. I'm engaged to marry him. I should never have—"

"Oh, come on, Louie. If you were in love with him, you wouldn't have gone with me."

"Not *if*, I *am* in love with him. I made a mistake. I won't do it again. And don't call me Louie."

He kept his eyes on her, not speaking for what seemed like a long time. She shared his gaze, wanting him to leave yet wanting him to stay.

"Why did you come today?" His voice was soft with no hint of accusation.

"Because you wrote to me and asked me to come so you could give me information important for my research."

"You could have asked me to mail it to you." His grin made him look boyish.

"Yes, I suppose I should have done that."

"But you didn't."

"Oh, Ben, stop it! Yes, I enjoy your company. I can't deny that, but I won't let it go any further than friendship. It's your turn to stop pretending that I will."

"Very well, Louisa Van Patten, I will not pressure you. I will leave you free to make your own mistakes." The hint of a grin on his face had not yet disappeared.

She wanted to tell him she had no intention of making more mistakes, and to insist that his implication that marrying Lemuel Ross would be a mistake was misguided;, but the waiter came to take their order, and she said nothing more about it. Afterward, she thought that to bring it up again would come across as too defensive. Instead, she asked him about the information he had promised.

"It looks as if you and your friend Mrs. Sanger may get your way regarding the eugenics movement. To say the least, it seems to be progressing."

She sat up straighter, her curiosity heightened. "What kind of progress?"

"There's going to be a test case for sterilization for certain undesirables, and I expect it will go all the way to the Supreme Court."

"I don't like that term, *undesirables*. They are deviants—epileptics, feebleminded, morally degenerate, but—"

"But you want to wipe them out by sterilization. And why would you do that if they aren't undesirable?"

"You're oversimplifying, but you know where I stand on this, and we've had this argument before. Let's not go over that ground again. Now tell me how you know this."

"Sources. Isn't that how we journalists learn everything?"

"Sources?"

"A source in the Virginia State Legislature. And, I confess, he's not really my source, but I have a buddy who works for the Richmond paper who knows him."

"Never mind that," Louisa said. "What's the Virginia legislature got to do with this?"

"There's a former state senator in Virginia who's on the board of the institution."

"The Colony, yes, I'm familiar with it."

"Well, this former senator, man by the name of Albert Strode, has drafted a bill to legalize sterilizing these deviants as you call them. I'm told he's already found an active senator to introduce it, and there's no question that it will pass."

"Did you say Albert Strode?"

"You know him?"

"Yes, Lemuel introduced me to him. We had dinner with him and another gentleman, Irving Whitehead, I believe. They are both quite interested in the eugenics movement."

"Ah, Lemuel. He's quite interested in the movement as well, I'm sure."

"He is, yes." She stiffened, remembering Lemuel had called it her *ridiculous little project.* "But why is this such important news?" she asked, resenting that Ben had made her feel defensive. "Other states have passed the same kind of laws and had them declared unconstitutional."

"Oh, but our friend Mr. Strode is aware of that. His bill, I'm told, takes care of all the problems embedded in other laws that rendered them unconstitutional. Besides that, he and the Colony are banking on a change of attitude and what he calls a better understanding on the part of the public regarding the laws of heredity. Just the thing you've been researching, isn't it?"

"Go on." Her voice was without warmth.

"Well, the bill's a shoo-in, my colleague's source says, and apparently this source knows since he's another state senator. Strode's already got a test case lined up. Some poor woman in that institution, I assume."

Louisa brightened. "Ben, that truly is interesting—and exciting. If I can include the testimony of a test trial in my book, it will add another dimension." Louisa paused a moment. "But why are you telling me this? You're on the opposite side of the fence. You don't believe in—"

"Doesn't matter what I believe," Ben said with a little laugh. "I knew you'd be interested. I knew it would be important for your research. Besides, what's wrong with helping out a friend? Even if she is on the other side of the fence."

"Thank you. I'm…I'm overwhelmed."

Ben smiled. "Not as much as I'd like," he said and then quickly changed the subject. "I'll be covering the trial if there is one. You could be an important source."

"I see."

"Don't take offense. I've given you some important advance information, and you may be able to help me in return. You'll be at the trial once it's set, won't you?"

"Of course." She managed a smile. "And to show you my appreciation for your information, lunch today is on me."

"My, my, quite the modern woman, aren't you? But I'm not a modern man. I'm terribly old-fashioned. Not sure I know how to handle a woman paying for my meal."

"You'll learn."

He laughed. "You are, as they say, the cat's pajamas."

"Oh no! You're trying to show me you're not so old-fashioned after all!"

"And you're going to tell me I'm not succeeding. I know, I know, by the time I learn some of your college-kid slang, it's already out of date."

"I don't think of you as old-fashioned," Louisa said, "and I don't like that you think of me as a college kid. I'm much more than that."

"You don't have to convince me how much more than that you are," he said as the waiter set their plates on the table and made a show of removing the silver covers.

Later, as they left the restaurant, Louisa was not surprised that he insisted on hailing a taxi to take her back to the train station. What did surprise her, though, was that after he had opened the taxi door for her, he pulled her close and kissed her on the mouth.

"Be seeing you," he said when he released her and walked away.

She stared after him until the cabbie barked, "Get in, lady."

To: Louisa Van Patten, Bryn Mawr College
From: Ben Newman, New York Times
October 1, 1924

Dear Louisa,

A quick note to let you know that a young woman has been selected for the sterilization test case in Virginia. Her name is Carrie Buck, an inmate at the Virginia Colony. Didn't you mention her name to me once? It is widely believed that Strode is going to base his arguments in part on the supposed principle that feeblemindedness and other deviancies are hereditary. He will try to show that the young woman is the daughter of a feebleminded woman and that she has had a feebleminded child. I know that is also part of the premise of your book.

All of this means that the legal proceedings are gaining momentum, and we can expect them to go to trial soon. I'm delighted! It means I'll see you again soon. In the meantime, I have a great deal of work to do.

Ben

To: Mr. and Mrs. J. T. Dobbs, Charlottesville, Virginia
From: Carolyn Wilhelm, Red Cross Secretary of Public Welfare,
Albemarle County, Virginia
October 15, 1924

Dear Mr. and Mrs. Dobbs:

I am writing to inform you that a representative from the State of Virginia and I will visit you on Tuesday for the purpose of assessing the child born to Carrie Buck, who was your ward and is now a resident of the Virginia State Colony for Epileptics and Feebleminded. You are to be prepared to exhibit the child and to answer questions regarding her mental capacity and welfare.

Sincerely,
Carolyn Wilhelm
Albemarle County Red Cross

24

ALICE

Alice Dobbs grumbled to herself as she read the letter she'd just brought in from the mailbox in front of her house. She'd seen immediately that it was from that Red Cross nurse who took Carrie off to the Colony. Now somebody was coming back to bother her by asking questions about Vivian.

Alice was beginning to wish she hadn't pushed J. T. so hard to get Carrie out of the house. She missed Carrie. The girl had been a big help with the chores, now left entirely to Alice. There was even more work to do now that there was a baby to care for. When she thought about it, Carrie wasn't really any trouble at all—except for getting pregnant when she wasn't married and embarrassing the family.

However, the way things turned out, nobody was putting shame on her and J. T. for what the girl had done. In fact, it was just the opposite. Everybody was saying how good it was of them to have kept the poor girl as long as they had and to have taken in little Vivian. Some even said it was probably some no-good man who took advantage of a poor girl. Alice always said she had no idea who it could have been.

This visit from someone to see Vivian just couldn't mean anything good. Alice wondered if they were thinking about taking Vivian away from her. It would be just like the government to do that now that she'd grown fond of the little thing. She'd always liked having babies around, and since Lucy's youngest was close to the same age, they'd be good playmates whenever Lucy and Tom came to visit. Lucy, in fact, was supposed to be at Alice's house tomorrow. She was coming without Tom and the other kids and just bringing the new baby for a visit. Alice had been looking forward to spending all day with the two of them and Vivian.

It was early afternoon the next day when the county-owned car came to a stop in front of the house. Lucy had arrived with her baby only a few minutes earlier and was in the bedroom nursing him while Vivian slept. Alice recognized the Red Cross nurse sitting in the passenger's seat. She watched from behind a curtain in the living room as a skinny man in a fancy suit got out and opened the door for the nurse. She moved away from the window and waited for several seconds after she heard the knock before she went to the door.

"Mrs. Dobbs," the nurse said, "I'm Caroline Wilhelm from the Red Cross, and this is Dr. DeJarnette. I believe you were expecting us."

Without answering, Alice moved aside to allow the two to enter. She'd already formed an opinion of the doctor. She didn't like the foreign sound of his name or the fact that he was so thin and long in the body. People like that reminded her of snakes. The two of them stood awkwardly in the living room until finally the nurse spoke.

"Is the baby here?" She checked a notebook in her hand quickly. "I believe her name is Vivian?"

"She's here," Alice said. "She's sleeping."

A frown crept across the snake's forehead. "Will you wake her, please? I have other duties to attend to."

"No, I ain't going to wake her," Alice told him. "Too hard to get her to go to sleep in the first place."

"I'm afraid you must, Mrs. Dobbs," the nurse said. She was ruffling the pages of her notebook in a nervous manner. "It is a requirement of the courts that we examine the child for signs of—"

"Hello," Lucy said, emerging from the bedroom with a baby on each hip. "I'm Lucy Pote. Are y'all the people Mama said had to check on Vivian?"

"We are," Dr. DeJarnette said in his clipped, irritated voice. "And we need to get on with it before the hour grows later."

"Why y'all doing this?" Lucy asked. Alice had wanted to ask the same question, but she was afraid that if she did, she would appear ignorant.

"It's required by the courts," Nurse Wilhelm said.

"Has something to do with the state putting Carrie in the Colony?" Lucy, it seemed, had no fear of asking questions. Alice hoped it didn't make them both appear ignorant.

"In a way, yes," the nurse said.

The doctor interrupted her before she could say more. "We are required to determine whether or not the child shows signs of feeblemindedness since that is a hereditary condition."

"Oh," Lucy said. She turned her side so Alice could take Vivian from her hip and cradled her own baby in her arms. "This is my baby here. His name is Thomas, and he's only a few weeks older than Vivian, but he's smart as a whip. I guarantee you that."

"Mrs. Dobbs, I'd like to get on with the test now," DeJarnette said, ignoring Lucy's obviously defensive bragging. "Have a seat there on the sofa with it in your lap, and I'll begin."

Alice noted the way he referred to Vivian as "it." Another reason to dislike him. Nevertheless she did as she was told, while Lucy sat in J. T.'s chair across from the sofa, holding Thomas in her lap. Both mother and baby looked on with curiosity until Thomas had enough of it and crinkled his face to cry out.

"He's kinda impatient when he's not busy," Lucy said apologetically. She pulled a celluloid rattle out of her pocket and gave it to Thomas. He shook it once or twice and threw it on the floor.

"A very active child, I see," Dr. DeJarnette said, looking at Lucy's baby. He turned his gaze to Vivian who was sucking her thumb and falling back on Alice's bosom, trying to go back to sleep.

"Oh yes!" Lucy said, reaching to retrieve the rattle. "He's active all right. Got a real curious mind."

Dr. DeJarnette pulled something from his pocket. Alice saw that it was a tiny wooden horse tied to a string. He dangled the horse in front of Vivian, who by this time had gone back to sleep and didn't react. When the doctor grasped her arm and shook it, Vivian woke with a start and began to cry. The doctor dangled the horse on the string with more force in front of her, but she seemed not to notice and fell back on Mrs. Dobbs's bosom with her eyes closed. When the doctor got up from the sofa to dangle the horse in front of Thomas, he reached for it, caught it on the second try, and immediately brought it to his mouth.

"No, no," Lucy said, grabbing the horse. "Not in your mouth."

"Normal reaction," the doctor said. "The mouth is often its main sensory organ."

Lucy gave him a puzzled look.

Dr. DeJarnette tried handing Vivian more toys, which she mostly ignored until she was finally awake enough to grab them. He looked into her eyes with a flashlight, irritating her to an even greater level, and then went behind the door and called out, "Hello," in a loud voice, startling both babies and making them cry. With each test, he mumbled something to the nurse, who dutifully wrote in her notebook.

The intrusion didn't last as long as Alice head feared. Nevertheless, she was glad to see the two of them leave.

25

LOUISA

The morning train trip from Charlottesville to Lynchburg had been pleasant for Louisa and Anne. Autumn had just taken its first bite out of summer, sucking out some of the dampness from the air and leaving it chewed up in clumps of gusty wind. Louisa, with the help of her professor and Irving Whitehead, had gotten permission from the superintendent of the Colony for a visit with Carrie as part of her research, and Anne had taken the day off from her duties as district nurse to accompany her.

"So, are the wedding plans still on?" Anne asked several miles into the journey.

Louisa gave her a surprised look. "Of course. Why wouldn't they be?"

"I don't know. I guess I was just remembering that you confided in me that Lemuel was a little upset with you at one point about your interest in your career to the exclusion of him and the wedding."

"Oh, that!" Louisa said with a wave of her hand. "It was just—"

"And then there was that question about Ben Newman you asked me .You've mentioned him several times, so I guess I just put two and two together and came up with a question."

Louisa laughed. "Your math is bad, Anne."

"Is it?"

"Yes. Lemuel and I had a little misunderstanding, that's all. And as for Ben, he happens to be interested in the eugenics movement from a journalist's standpoint, as well as the bill the Virginia legislature passed, so of course he would contact me."

"Of course he would." There was teasing sarcasm in Anne's voice.

"Oh, come on, Anne. Don't be that way. I haven't discouraged Ben's contacting me because he has all of his *sources*, as he calls them. Turns out they provide valuable information for my work as well as for his newspaper stories."

"Mmm-hmm," Anne said and laughed.

"Stop it, Anne!" Louisa said, but Anne's laughter was contagious. Louisa couldn't suppress her own laugh before she added, "I really am grateful for the help Ben has given me. I thought you'd see that. I thought you wanted me to succeed with this book."

"Of course I do," Anne said, sobering only a little. "And I want you to succeed with Lemuel, too. Or Ben. Or whomever you might decide upon."

Louisa shook her head and smiled. "You're impossible."

Before Anne could reply, the conductor announced that they were approaching the Lynchburg station and asked them to prepare to disembark. A driver from the Colony met them at the station. By the time they reached Madison Heights and the red-brick building that housed the superintendent's office, Louisa had grown quiet, and Anne, sensing her tension, had stopped her teasing.

Dr. Priddy, the superintendent, was not in the office, but he had arranged for them to be immediately escorted to the building where Carrie lived and worked.

Louisa could feel the heat emanating from the kitchen as they approached. It flowed from a door opening into a long dining hall, swallowing up all vestiges of the crisp autumn air. She could see Carrie in the kitchen, lifting a large and obviously heavy steaming pot from the stove to a counter. She then bent down to pull another large pan from an oven to be placed on the counter. Moving quickly, she grabbed a knife and sliced onions into the pan and then, with the same fast movement, lifted another large, steaming pot from the stove.

Once Louisa entered the kitchen, the heat wrapped its heavy arms around her with such closeness that she found breathing difficult. There was so much noise in the kitchen that Carrie didn't hear the escort when she called out to her, and the woman had to resort to going to her and touching her arm. Carrie turned her damp, flushed face toward her with a startled expression. She glanced toward Louisa and Anne when the escort pointed to them and allowed herself to be led out of the kitchen with them.

"They just want to talk to you," the escort told her. "You can sit over there at that corner table."

Carrie nodded but didn't speak. Her eyes were dull, and she looked too old to be only eighteen. Her hair, where it had slipped out of the white kerchief on her head, was wet and plastered to her forehead. Dampness made her reddened face glisten.

"Do you remember me, Carrie?" Louisa asked after they were seated.

"Yes, ma'am. I remember you and Nurse Harris both," she said, glancing at Anne.

"A lot has happened since I saw you last," Louisa said.

"I reckon that's right." Carrie wiped her sweating face with her apron, leaving the apron with a dark smudge.

"You've had a baby."

Carrie brightened a little. "Her name's Annabelle."

"Annabelle? I understood her name was Vivian."

"Her name's Annabelle."

"I see," Louisa said, noting the hard look that had come over the girl's face. She was certain Mrs. Dobbs had told her the baby's name was Vivian. Perhaps Carrie had forgotten. A manifestation of feeblemindedness? "And you've been admitted to the Colony, of course," Louisa added.

Carrie shrugged. "They said it was for my own good."

"And it is, of course," Louisa said. "Your mother is here as well, I believe. That must make you happy."

"Makes my mama happy. Being here, I mean. She likes it here. But for myself, I'd rather be out of here like I was before."

Louisa saw her opening. "There is a chance you can be released eventually, Carrie." She glanced at Anne as if for confirmation, but Anne said nothing and only looked miserable from the heat. "Have you been told about that possibility?" Louisa asked, turning back to Carrie.

"Oh they told me, all right. Something about an operation. They asked me if had anything to say about what they want to do."

"And what did you tell them?" Louisa felt her breath quicken and wished she could have had a stenographer with her since Carrie was so willing to talk.

"I told them what Mama told me to tell them. That I was going to leave everything up to my people."

"Your people?" Louisa frowned. "Who are your people?"

"The ones that took over and put me here. Mama said I should say I'd leave it up to them because they know what's best for me."

"Do you think they know what's best for you?" Louisa asked.

"I don't know. All I know is that I never had a epileptic fit in my life and neither did my mama, so I don't know why they—"

Anne leaned forward, speaking for the first time. "Carrie, the Colony is not just for epileptics. It's for people with other forms of feeble..." She stopped speaking when Louisa moved her hand toward her in a cautionary manner.

"What were you saying, Carrie?" Louisa asked.

Carrie shrugged again. "I know they told me that if I have that operation I can probably get out of here."

"Do you understand what the operation is?" Louisa asked.

"Not really. Kind of like having my appendix out, they said."

Louisa glanced at Anne with a look of alarm on her face. "Is that what they told you?" she asked, turning back to Carrie.

"They said it wasn't very serious. That it was kind of like having your appendix taken out."

"Carrie, it's not—"

"Louisa," Anne interrupted. "it's not wise to go into too much detail. The policy in this kind of situation is not to cause undue stress."

"She has a right to know!" She glared at Anne.

"Know what?" Carrie asked.

Louisa turned back to Carrie. "If you have the operation, you won't be able to have any more children."

Carrie was silent for a long time, rolling and unrolling the hem of her smudged apron. "They didn't tell me that," she said finally. She looked up, her eyes glistening. "I always wanted to have two or three kids." She sighed, and her eyes seemed to lose focus for a few seconds before she fixed her gaze on Louisa again. "But they said if I don't have the operation, I'll never get out of here."

"I know it's hard for you to understand," Louisa said, "but—"

"I understand!" Carrie's voice had a sharpness Louisa had never heard before. "They think I'm feebleminded. They think I can't take care of my baby. I see now that they want to fix me so I can't have any more that they think I can't take care of. Maybe they're right. I don't know. I reckon there's lots I don't know, 'cept that it's time I got back to work." She stood up abruptly and walked back to the kitchen.

The interview and visit with Carrie left Louisa unsettled— Carrie's sickly appearance, the evidence of backbreaking work under deplorable conditions, and the fact that the purpose of the operation hadn't been explained to her. The most disturbing of all, however, was Carrie's intelligent response to her situation. She had reasoned out what she had to do—reasoned in a way that a feeble-minded person would not be able to do.

When Louisa confided her unease to Anne, she'd told her not to be concerned. She'd seen plenty of feebleminded people who could be rational at times, and Louisa should have confidence in the tests administered by professionals that had proved Carrie feebleminded.

Anne's words were of no comfort to Louisa and did nothing to alleviate the nagging feeling that Carrie had been misdiagnosed and perhaps should not be in an institution like the Virginia State Colony for Epileptics and Feebleminded. She consoled herself with the knowledge that tomorrow she would be with Lemuel. She could talk to him about her doubts. He would have a wise response. Certainly it would be something more than Anne's admonition simply not to be concerned.

Lemuel paid for her train trip from Charlottesville to Richmond and was to meet her at the station when she arrived. When Louisa stepped off the train, she looked around anxiously but didn't see him. He had always met her outside on the platform, standing a distance back so he could see passengers departing all of the cars in order to rush to her immediately.

The station was a glass-eyed monster that sucked passengers into its innards where, once consumed, they moved in a sluggish turmoil. Louisa moved with the crowd to the inside and felt a twinge of despair when she still didn't see Lemuel. Was she to join the tumult to look for him? Or wait for him to find her? Should she take a taxi instead to the Ross home? His mother was supposedly waiting for her to stay overnight after they had dinner at home. Had she come on the wrong day? It would be embarrassing to show up at the wrong time. But what was she to do?

Someone called her name. "Miss Van Patten!" She swung around to see a young man rushing toward her. "Miss Van Patten!" He stopped in front of her, out of breath. He was dressed in a wrinkled blue suit, an equally wrinkled white shirt, and an inexpertly knotted brown tie.

"I'm Louisa Van Patten," she said.

"Oh, forgive me, please, Miss. I know I'm late, but my car...It wouldn't start and... Well, here I am. Mr. Ross sent me to meet you, and he described you perfectly. He said you would be the prettiest...Oh, forgive me," he said again, blushing this time. "I'm Marcus Wallace, Mr. Ross's assistant. He sent me here. I'm to take you to his mother's house."

"He sent you here? Why didn't he come himself?"

"An important matter. Real estate, a merger. And there was a meeting with the principals. Money involved, you see. A lot of it, I think. Well, I don't know if I should have...He said to tell you he'd explain it to you. Said he'd meet you at his mother's house. Said it would give you time to change, and...Oh, it's not that you don't look lovely already, but, well, anyway..." He blushed again and said he would get a porter to help with her bags. Then he left her standing while he went to fetch one.

Louisa waited, feeling slightly awkward, while Marcus managed to get her bags loaded into his car and came back into the station to fetch her.

"Well, Marcus," she said as she settled into the passenger seat next to him, "I wasn't aware that Lemuel, I mean Mr. Ross, had an assistant."

"I'm new," Marcus said. "Mr. Ross's firm is growing, and I'm studying law at the university, so when he advertised for an assistant, I was one of the dozens who applied. I mean, it's expensive, don't you know. Law school, I mean, and I don't come from a wealthy...Well, as I said, dozens of us applied. Everyone wants to work there because the firm is growing and making so much money. Oh, forgive me. Maybe I shouldn't talk about money to a lady. It's just that I'm not used to being around...Well, what I mean is, I think you'll be pleased to know that Mr. Ross is so successful."

"Of course," Louisa said. "But you don't suppose this meeting he's in is going to last several hours."

"Oh no. He said to tell you it would only be an hour at the most."

"An hour? I see. I suppose when a lot of money is involved, it takes time."

"Oh yes, it does. And I'm so lucky to be the one he chose to... Well, what I mean is I'm learning so much. Mr. Ross has a very keen mind for business and the law. But I suppose you know that, or maybe you don't. Women don't have much interest in such—"

"I have a great deal of interest in everything Lemuel does."

"Oh, of course you do." Marcus squirmed in his seat. "I didn't mean to imply...No, what I mean is..."

Louisa felt near exhaustion from Marcus's nervous chatter by the time they reached the Ross mansion. The fact that a butler met them at the door seemed to embarrass Marcus. For some reason he found it necessary to take his leave by backing away and bowing to the butler. He was even more embarrassed when he backed into a doorjamb. He didn't seem to be seriously injured, however, and the butler helped him through the door before he showed Louisa into Mrs. Ross's reception room.

Mrs. Ross rose from her Queen Anne chair next to the fireplace and set the book she'd been reading open and face down on a table when Louisa entered. Louisa was surprised to see that she had changed her hairstyle to a short marcel wave. She managed to appear fashionable but still elegant in her ankle-length dress of heavy gray silk.

"Oh, Louisa, my dear, it's so good to see you. It's been too long," she said, opening her arms to embrace Louisa.

"It's wonderful to see you as well," Louisa said, brushing her cheek with a kiss.

"Please have a seat, and we'll have tea while we wait for Lem." Mrs. Ross made small talk about the weather and how difficult it was to keep the large house warm. When the tea arrived, she changed the subject to Louisa. "You must tell me about your progress on your book, Louisa. I've asked Lem, but he only gives the vaguest of answers."

"I'm quite busy with the research," Louisa said, wondering why Lemuel's answers had been vague. She'd kept him abreast of everything. "There will be a trial soon, here in Virginia, that will help determine the future of the eugenics movement nationally, but you must know about that."

"Oh, I'm afraid I don't know about it," Mrs. Ross said, "but it will no doubt be important for your research."

"Oh yes, very important," Louisa said. "I'll be attending the trial, of course."

"Oh my!" Mrs. Ross said, sitting back in her chair. "How very daring but exciting, too, I should say."

Louisa smiled and took a sip of her tea, not certain why Mrs. Ross would think attending a trial was daring. She was a southern lady, though, and they seemed to cling to their old-fashioned ways.

Perhaps that was why Lemuel had been vague with her about the book.

"Oh, I see you're reading *A Passage to India*," Louisa said, grateful that she'd seen the novel on a chairside table. "Are you enjoying it?"

"What? Oh yes, very much so. I envy the young heroine all of her adventures, but please don't change the subject, dear. I really do want to hear more about your work and this trial you mentioned."

Louisa was chagrined that Mrs. Ross had foiled her attempt, and she felt a moment of uncertainty. But if the lady asked for details, wouldn't it be rude to refuse her? She took a deep breath. "Well, you see, the trial is to determine whether or not it is legal to sterilize individuals who are feebleminded or epileptic."

Mrs. Ross's eyes, alight with little fires, were set on Louisa. She said nothing for a few seconds until finally she managed, "I see." After another second or two, she spoke again. "To keep them from producing more feebleminded persons or epileptics."

"Exactly. You see, scientific research indicates those traits are hereditary."

"Oh," Mrs. Ross said. It was an enigmatic *oh*, implying perhaps enlightened surprise, perhaps doubt. Or could it be disappointment? Louisa wasn't sure what to say, but Mrs. Ross saved her the trouble. "If I remember correctly, you are attempting to interpret the minds of your subjects who may be deviant in certain ways."

"Yes, that's right!" Louisa couldn't hide her pleasure that Mrs. Ross remembered such detail.

"And feeblemindedness, epilepsy, that sort of thing would fit your subject."

"Yes, and since moral deviancy is common in that type of person, I hope to gain some understanding as to why."

"Interesting," Mrs. Ross said. "You modern girls are certainly branching out. Such freedom as I've never known."

"I understand that. My own mother also lacked the freedom I have."

"I'm not sure Lem understands all of the implications." The flame in her eyes had retreated behind a smoky veil.

Louisa was stunned. Was Mrs. Ross hinting that her work could cause problems in her marriage to Lemuel?

"I don't mean to be interfering, my dear. It's just that I sensed a bit of disappointment from you when I mentioned that Lem hadn't been very specific about your work. Don't let that surprise you. It's the nature of men to be self-centered. It's that attitude that makes them our protectors and our benefactors. My dear late husband, Lem's father, was the same way, and I wouldn't be surprised to hear that your own father has similar characteristics. Oh, I'll admit, it does make us feel unappreciated and belittled at times," she said, holding up her small, delicate hand as if to fend off an attack, "but don't let those feelings overtake you. It's the way of the world, my dear. It doesn't mean that they love us any less. It's just that they know they must come first."

"Surely Lemuel hasn't suggested to you that I should forsake—"

"He has suggested nothing, and certainly not that you forsake your interest in this matter," Mrs. Ross said. "Don't you see, my dear, I'm simply warning you not to feel too disappointed if he doesn't show the enthusiasm you might be seeking from him. He loves you with all of his heart. Surely you know that."

"Yes, I know that," Louisa said. It was the kind of thing her mother might have said, except her own mother would not have acknowledged that there was any merit to the work she was doing as Mrs. Ross had. It seemed clear to Louisa that Mrs. Ross was fond of her. Maybe she would do well to listen to her.

When a bell sounded, Mrs. Ross sat up straighter and her eyes regained their light. "Oh, that must be Lem."

Within a few seconds he entered the room. Louisa noticed the dark circles under his eyes and the tired, drawn look of his face.

"What a treat to see two beautiful women waiting for me," he said. He moved toward Louisa and bent to kiss her on the cheek and then kissed his mother's cheek. "So sorry to keep you waiting, but there was work I had to do." He perched himself on the arm of Louisa's chair and caressed her shoulders lightly.

"We're happy you're here, late or not," Mrs. Ross said, smiling at her son. "But if you will indulge your mother and allow her to be motherly, I must say you're working too much these days."

"You always say that," Lemuel said with a little laugh. He got up from his spot next to Louisa and sprawled on a sofa. "I hope dinner can wait long enough for a Scotch and soda," he said.

A frown creased Mrs. Ross's elegant brow. "Lem, you know Scotch and soda is out of the question. There's a law against it, and it could ruin your career if—"

"I know, I know. Prohibition's the law of the land, but there's nothing like Scotch to help a man relax, and I happen to know you still have Papa's stash in the basement. And don't worry about it ruining my career," he added with a little laugh. "Anyone with the power to do that is probably sitting by the fire sipping his own Scotch and soda."

Louisa saw Mrs. Ross glance at the butler waiting by the door and saw the slight rise of her chin. Within a few minutes, the butler delivered the drink to Lemuel on a silver tray. Louisa felt a pang of guilt, remembering the gin she'd consumed with Ben. She did her best to push the guilt aside and listen as Lemuel regaled the two women with a story about a judge whom he recently had to rescue from a local speakeasy. Lemuel helped him stagger out the door and then covered him with an overcoat to get him through a public parking lot to a waiting car. His story of the judge's stumbles and drunken remarks made both Louisa and Mrs. Ross laugh, but Louisa's laugh was subdued. His mention of a speakeasy had stabbed her with more guilt.

"And now, my dear," Lemuel said, turning to Louisa, after his first taste of the Scotch, "you must tell me about your academic adventures."

"Oh yes, much has happened. You must have heard about the trial. Your friend Mr. Strode will be representing the Colony at Lynchburg."

"Aubrey? I knew he was the lawyer for that institution of epileptics and the like, but I haven't heard about any trial."

"The presumption that feeblemindedness and epilepsy are hereditary will be part of the state's argument that Mr. Strode will make, and that will be important to the development of my book."

"Of course," Lemuel said, taking another sip of his drink. He was beginning to look much more relaxed.

"The trial is really terribly important to me, and I am hoping you'll come to Lynchburg with me. Your legal mind would be such a benefit for me. You can give me blow-by-blow interpretations." Louisa knew she sounded excited, and she had truly meant to wait until they were alone to ask Lemuel to accompany her, but the moment seemed so right. Besides, Mrs. Ross had shown herself to be so supportive that Louisa was sure it didn't matter that they were not alone.

"Louisa, my dear, I couldn't possibly get away for such a thing. Not now, with this real estate deal in such a critical place. There's a lot of money involved, darling, so I'm sure you wouldn't want me to walk out on that."

"The trial isn't scheduled until November. That should work out perfectly for us." Louisa was still letting her enthusiasm show.

Lemuel chuckled. "These negotiations take months, darling. The more money that's involved, the longer it takes. Just ask Mother. She's been through this before."

Louisa glanced at Mrs. Ross who said nothing, but there was a slight, sympathetic smile on her lips. She looked at Lemuel again, who was now telling another anecdote—something about the other party in the real estate deal misinterpreting real estate law. Louisa said nothing more. She was wondering now if she should bring up the other matter she wanted to discuss with Lemuel: the fact that she was having doubts that Carrie's diagnosis was viable.

Perhaps not, she thought. Perhaps it wasn't important—at least not to Lemuel.

26

LOUISA

The year was dying in a cold, gray November fog while geese honked a funeral hymn over the James River. Louisa stood outside the Amherst County courthouse in her fur-collared, ankle-length coat with her hands warmed by a muff of matching fur, waiting for the courthouse to open. She had hoped to meet Anne Harris there, but Anne had written that since she was to be a witness in the Carrie Buck trial, she would be sequestered in a room in the courthouse.

Ben Newman was nowhere in sight either, although he had seemed eager to attend the trial when Louisa last heard from him by letter a month ago. She had purposely not contacted him, reminding herself with increasing chagrin that she should have never fostered such an intimate friendship with him. Lemuel was to be her husband. If she was to deserve him, she must act accordingly.

A cold breeze stirred the last sad residuals of what had been a blazing orange and red display on the trees, causing Louisa to hunch her shoulders and dig her hands deeper into the fur. The cold made her miserable; she was shivering and felt dizzy. As she silently cursed whoever had locked the courthouse doors, they suddenly were flung open by a middle-aged man dressed in a dark suit stretched tightly across an expanded stomach. Several other people, obviously as anxious as she was to get out of the cold, entered ahead of her. Once inside, they were directed to turn left to find the courtroom.

Louisa saw a table near the front where Carrie, looking pale and frightened, sat with two men. One was the balding and chubby Irving Whitehead, to whom Lemuel had introduced her. That surprised her. Was he to be Carrie's lawyer? Wouldn't that mean a conflict of interest since he was on the board of directors for the Colony? She didn't recognize the other man. At a table on the other side of the courtroom sat Aubrey Strode and Dr. Priddy. Louisa found a place to sit on the end of one of the benches near the front. It was warm, almost too warm, inside the courtroom, and she removed her coat. As she settled into the seat, she was still shaking slightly in spite of the warmth. That happened sometimes when she was nervous or overly excited. She took a few deep breaths, and the dizziness and shaking abated.

There was a low buzz of voices in the room, but Louisa hardly noticed them as she concentrated on Carrie, wondering how she felt, wondering if she was fully aware of what was happening. She was startled when someone sat beside her in the empty space next to the aisle but relieved and pleased when she saw it was Ben. He would be a poor substitute for Lemuel in helping her interpret the trial, but he was at least more knowledgeable than most.

"Sorry I'm late," he whispered. "I was doing some research, and it took me longer than I expected."

Louisa wasn't surprised at his excuse, but she was curious. "What kind of research?"

"The two lawyers. Strode and Whitehead. They're old friends."

"Yes, I know. I've met both of them," she said. "Surely you're not surprised that lawyers who are friends in private life often oppose each other in court."

"Not surprised, but in this case, a little more than curious. They both have ties to the Colony. Whitehead's even got a building named for him. He used to be a member of the board of directors."

"Yes, I know. And I must say I was surprised when I saw him there. My first thought was that it could be a conflict of interest."

"My thought as well. In fact, I wrote about it in one of the pieces that got cut by an editor."

Ben was interrupted by the voice of the bailiff telling everyone to rise as the judge entered the courtroom and took his seat at the bench. The judge called the court to order, and Whitehead asked that the record show the appellant was present. He introduced the appellant, the other man at the table, as R. G. Shelton, guardian for Carrie Buck. It struck Louisa how frightened and confused Carrie must have been to have two men she didn't know representing her at a trial that, no matter the outcome, would have a profound effect on her life.

Aubrey Strode stood, as handsome and poised as Louisa remembered him, and called his first witness, Anne Harris. She came to the stand looking tense but not frightened. She answered all the questions Strode asked her, telling the court that she'd known both Carrie and her mother, Emma, for twelve years and that she knew Emma's other children as well. She testified that Emma was irresponsible and either could not or would not take care of herself and her children, and they lived mostly on the streets. She also told Strode and the court that she believed Emma's children to be illegitimate.

"Are you familiar with the term *socially inadequate person*?" Strode asked.

"Yes sir," Anne replied. "It's a person who is not able to take care of themselves—who is irresponsible mentally."

"Now, you say Emma is irresponsible mentally?" Strode asked.

Anne answered yes, and Louisa knew where this was leading. Strode was trying to establish that the socially or mentally inadequate trait was passed from generation to generation. When he asked if Emma's children were mentally normal, Anne answered no. She said that all of them were four or five years younger mentally than their chronological age. Louisa felt a twinge of discomfort. Carrie didn't fit the description of being mentally below her chronological age, and she wondered how Anne could have come to such a sweeping conclusion.

Whitehead's cross-examination went over more or less the same ground, except that he got Anne to admit that she'd had very little contact with Carrie and knew little about her.

"You know nothing about her after the Dobbses took her?" Whitehead asked.

"Except one time," Anne said. She had not lost her tense expression. "That was when she was in grammar school and the superintendent called me and said she was having trouble with Carrie writing notes. That sort of thing. She asked what she should do about it."

"Writing notes. To boys, I suppose?" Whitehead said.

"Yes sir."

"Is writing notes to boys in school at the age of nine or ten considered antisocial?"

"For a child ten years old to write the notes she was writing, I should say so."

Louisa had seen the notes in question when Anne allowed her to read Carrie's files. She had considered them innocuous. She'd assumed Anne had as well.

Whitehead asked Anne if a girl sixteen years old had written the note, would it have been considered antisocial?

"Well, if a girl of sixteen had written that kind of note, she ought to have been sent to a correctional facility." Louisa was shocked. Anne had never even hinted that she found Carrie to be a problem in any way.

After Anne, three teachers testified about what they considered the low mental ability of Carrie's siblings. Ben scribbled a note and handed it to Louisa. *Why didn't Whitehead call one of Carrie's teachers? Especially if you say she wrote favorable notes on the report cards.*

Louisa didn't respond to his note. She was asking herself the same question though and feeling uneasy. If Carrie was inadequately represented, not only would it be unfair to her, but the story of the trial also would do nothing to enhance her book.

The testimony of all of the following witnesses surprised Louisa.

They were neighbors of some of Emma's family. None of them knew Carrie, and none of them could be persuaded to admit that the family members were mentally inadequate, only that some of them may have been "peculiar." Had Strode hoped they'd be more specific?

The next witness was Caroline Wilhelm. She testified that she had met Carrie after the hearing to have her committed to the Colony and that Carrie was pregnant and unmarried at the time.

"From your experience as a social worker, if Carrie were discharged from the Colony still capable of child-bearing, would she be likely to become the parent of deficient offspring?" Strode asked. Louisa noticed Ben sit up straighter, as if he disapproved of the question.

"I should judge so," Miss Wilhelm said. "I think a girl of her mentality is more or less at the mercy of other people, and this girl particularly, from her past record. Her mother had three illegitimate children, and I should say that Carrie would be very likely to have illegitimate children."

She's not qualified to say that! Whitehead should object! Ben scribbled quickly on a note he passed to Louisa.

"So the only way that she could likely be kept from increasing her own kind would be by either segregation or something that would stop her power to propagate. Is she an asset or a liability to society?"

That question was the crux of the trial and one of the most important aspects of Louisa's research. When Miss Wilhelm answered that Carrie would be a liability to society, Louisa was almost certain the trial would confirm her research.

In the next line of questioning, Strode asked about Miss Wilhelm's impression of Carrie's child.

"It's difficult to judge probabilities of a child as young as that, but it seems to me she's not quite a normal baby," she said. Strode asked her to explain. "In its appearance—I should say that perhaps my knowledge of the mother may prejudice me in that regard, but

I saw the child at the same time as Mrs. Dobbs's grandson, which is only three days older than this one, and there is a very decided difference in the babies."

"You would not judge the child of Carrie Buck as a normal baby?" Strode asked.

Miss Wilhelm nodded slowly. "There's a look about it that's not quite normal, but just what it is, I can't say."

Ben leaned forward in his seat when Whitehead began the cross-examination. After several questions that repeated Strode's questions, he finally got to his point.

"Are there any records down in Charlottesville in connection with social work that would tend to show that Carrie Buck was feebleminded or unsocial or antisocial or whatever the term is, other than the birth of her child?"

"No sir, our record begins on the seventeenth of January of this year, and that is the first knowledge we have of her."

Whitehead continued with a rambling question. "Basing your opinion that the girl is unsocial or antisocial on the fact she had an illegitimate child? The point I'm getting at is this: Are you basing your opinion on that?"

Miss Wilhelm nodded. "On that fact and that, as a social worker, I know that girls of this type—"

"What is the type?" Whitehead asked sharply, and Ben leaned forward even more.

"I should say decidedly feebleminded" came the reply.

"But the question of pregnancy is not evidence of feeblemindedness, is it? The fact that, as we say, she made a misstep—went wrong—is that evidence of feeblemindedness?"

"No, but a feebleminded girl is much more likely to go wrong."

"One more question," Whitehead said. "You said in answer to Colonel Strode that the girl was a decided liability. Do you mean this girl was taken care of by Mr. Dobbs and his family?"

"Yes sir."

"Up to the time she gave birth to this child?"

"Yes sir," Miss Wilhelm answered again.

At the same time, Ben leaned back in his seat and mumbled, "What the hell?"

Whitehead's questioning continued, getting Miss Wilhelm to testify that Carrie was capable of doing housework, but only under supervision, and that she would be less of a liability to the state if she were sterilized because it would prevent what she called "the propagation of her kind."

Whitehead summed up her testimony by saying, "Your idea is while she would never become an asset, she would become less of a liability by sterilization, and your idea is that she could be turned over to somebody and, under careful supervision, be made self-supporting. Is that your idea?"

"I think so. Yes sir," Miss Wilhelm said.

The last witness before the noon recess was the social worker whom Miss Wilhelm had replaced. She testified that, although she had seen Carrie only once and had never spoken to her, she considered her to be "not bright." Whitehead made no cross-examination.

"It's a damned kangaroo court," Ben said as he took Louisa's arm to escort her out of the courtroom.

"Shhh," Louisa warned. "Someone will hear you."

"Come on, I'll buy you lunch someplace where I can say anything I want," Ben said.

Louisa hesitated. "Ben, I...I don't think I—"

"I'm not going to seduce you," Ben said, "and yes I know you're still feeling guilty about our night out, but I didn't seduce you then, did I?"

"Well... She felt decidedly uncomfortable that he could guess how guilty she felt.

"This is a business lunch, Louisa," he said, taking her arm again to lead her away from the courthouse. "It's to help clarify things for your book."

"Well, you've done it again," she said with a little laugh as they settled into a booth at a nearby restaurant. "You've led me astray."

"You're flirting with me," he said.

"Never," she said. "This is a business lunch."

"They're feeding your girl to the wolves," he said, looking at the menu. He was at least pretending not to notice that she was blushing.

"Surely not on purpose," she said.

Ben raised an eyebrow. "Oh, I think it's on purpose. The Colony wants her sterilized, and so does her lawyer, who, as we both know, has close ties to the Colony."

"He's made at least an attempt at defending her rights, don't you think?"

Ben laughed derisively. "He hasn't made any such attempt. He's just putting on a show. Why didn't he follow up on that social worker's claim that a feebleminded girl is much more likely to go wrong? He could have discredited her because she had just admitted that getting pregnant out of wedlock isn't evidence of feeblemindedness. He should have made her explain that statement in regard to Carrie. He just let it go and went on with his leading questions to get her to confirm that Carrie has always been a liability to society."

"Well, I can see that he did do that," Louisa said. She didn't want to admit to how unsettled she felt.

"He tried to get the social worker to say that sterilization would deter immorality, but when he couldn't do that, he summarized her testimony in the wording the state might have used. He, in fact, made the case for the state."

"Then how do you think he ended up as Carrie's lawyer?"

"I think the Colony chose him."

"What?"

"I can't prove it yet, but I believe they did. I think they knew he wouldn't do anything to mess up their conviction that the so-called feebleminded and epileptic need to be sterilized."

"Nevertheless, I still fail to see why you can't see the advantages of that," Louisa said. "A society without feebleminded and epileptics and other deviants would be a greater society."

"Don't give me your 'nevertheless.' If this is to be a legitimate decision, it has to be decided in a legitimate court. Besides, I've asked you before, who gets to decide who's a deviant?"

"Isn't it obvious?"

"No, it's not," Ben said. "Remember, I told you I was late because I'd been doing some research? Well, let me tell you just smidgen of what I found out. The illustrious Aubrey Strode—"

"He's an excellent lawyer," Louisa interrupted. "Surely you won't refute that."

"He's an excellent lawyer, indeed. He's done a great deal of good for Virginia, things like drafting legislation to establish the state health department, the parole and probation system, and all those programs to help poor children get an education. Not to mention how he's promoted college education for women, but who's to say he's not a deviant?"

Louisa laughed derisively. "You must be joking."

"Both his mother and father were deemed insane."

"What?"

"They each died in state institutions."

Louisa felt as if the blood had drained from her body. "There could have been extenuating circumstances. Disease or...I remember he mentioned that his father was a university president, and his mother was—"

"I'm sure they were both accomplished citizens, and of course, there could have been extenuating circumstances. As I said, who's to say? I do know, however, that his parents' histories with insanity almost kept him from getting an insurance policy. Whitehead probably knew all about it, but the Colony knew he wouldn't mention it."

"This sounds a bit like gossip to me, and I don't know how you can possibly dig up these things," Louisa said.

Ben chuckled. "Trust me, it's well-documented. Speaking of gossip, listen to this: An old friend of Strode's told me that when the two of them were young, Strode kept getting letters from a girlfriend who claimed she was pregnant and that he was the father. Turned out she wasn't pregnant, but Strode apparently admitted it was a possibility, and before that, he told her she was on her own if she was pregnant by him. Couldn't afford to ruin his political future, apparently."

Louisa shook her head. "What awful things you turn up."

"Yes, awful. But apparently it's not quite so awful if you happen to be the male in the affair or if you happen to be from the right side of the tracks."

"I see your point," she said. No longer hungry, she stared out the window, trying to sort out everything.

"Are you all right?" Ben asked.

"No," she said, turning toward him. "I'm full of doubts. They were already forming before the trial. I don't think there's anything at all wrong with Carrie's mind. I mean anyone can make a mistake in the heat of passion."

"Some do," Ben said. "Some are very careful."

Louisa let his insinuating remark pass. "No matter what my doubts may be about Carrie, and about this trial, I'm still convinced that sterilization for the betterment of the race and of society is the right thing to do," she said.

"The expert witnesses will be on the stand when the court reconvenes. They're supposed to convince the judge of that." He shook his head. "But I can guarantee their testimony will be a sham. At least one of them will be."

Louisa waited for him to continue. Finally, she said, "Are you going to tell me what you mean by that?"

"You'll say it's gossip."

"Is it?" she asked.

"No," he answered. "It's documented."

"Then tell me."

"You've heard of Harry Laughlin."

"Of course. He's one of the most prominent eugenicists at the Eugenics Record Office on Long Island. I know him well. He was the first to make the argument that compulsive sterilization rests on the same legal principle as mandatory vaccinations."

"Oh yes, he's adamant about sterilizing deviants. I believe he includes a number of categories—tramps, deaf, blind, physically deformed, and of course, the insane, feebleminded, and epileptic."

"I know that. What's your point?"

"Laughlin is epileptic."

Louisa found it difficult to breathe. "You're certain?" she finally asked.

"Of course, I'm certain. I wouldn't have mentioned it if I wasn't."

"But how did you—?"

"I have sources. I told you that."

"It's completely unethical to look into another's health records." She was becoming increasingly irritated with him and even felt for a moment as if she might faint.

"I'm sure Carrie would agree with you."

"Nevertheless," she said, shaking her head, "I happen to know Harry Laughlin is an extremely intelligent man."

"I didn't say he wasn't intelligent; I said he's epileptic."

"But it's been shown that the minds of epileptics deviate from the norm to the extent of degrees of insanity," she said.

"Apparently not all of them. Apparently we don't know as much about insanity and feeblemindedness and epilepsy as we should."

"Of course there's always more to learn, but—"

"Another one of the witnesses will be your friend Estabrook," Ben said, interrupting her. "He's sure to go on and on about his study of the family Juke and the family Nam and all their feeble-mindedness, but he won't mention any of the family members who've excelled."

Louisa covered her eyes and face with the palms of her hands for a brief moment, as much to assuage her dizziness as to get her thoughts in order. Ben was referring to Estabrook's extensive research of families with several members who were considered deviant. "I know Dr. Estabrook didn't mention those who were normal in the families he studies," she said, bringing her hands to her lap. "The point is that there is a preponderance of deviants in those families. And I still believe that society will benefit by ridding itself of deviants—those who are unfit and should never reproduce themselves."

Ben was silent, for a long time, looking at her. Finally he asked, "I ask yet again, who gets to decide who's unfit and why?"

27

LOUISA

The testimony from expert witnesses mostly dealt with scientific studies of genetics and heredity. Louisa listened with great interest to all of it. Ben sat beside her taking notes. By Louisa's count, Strode called eleven witnesses to prove his point that Carrie was mentally defective and that she had inherited it from her mother and passed it on to her child. Her lawyer, Irving Whitehead, called no witnesses at all.

"Why didn't he argue that the new sterilization law violated the constitution?" Ben asked at the end of the trial. "Why didn't he argue that it deprived her of equal protection under the law? Why the hell did he keep making the point that sterilization would be good for her? I tell you why. It's because this was a goddamned setup. Whitehead was hired by the Colony!"

"Will you write all that in your story?" Louisa's head was beginning to ache, and she couldn't keep the weariness out of her voice.

"Damn right, I will," Ben said. "The question is will the paper print the story? So far they've refused to print a lot of the stuff I've dug up."

"Why?" Louisa asked.

Ben shrugged. "Who knows? Are they afraid of a libel suit? Did somebody buy 'em?"

Ben's train back to New York left ahead of Louisa's, and it was several weeks before she heard from him again. At the end of February, a telegram for her from Ben arrived. Its message was simple. The judge had decided in favor of the State of Virginia. Appeals would follow.

Louisa felt a jolt of despair. She told herself it wasn't that she no longer believed in the principles of sterilization for the purification of the race; it was because Ben and her own observation had convinced her that Carrie's defense had been inadequate. She felt compelled to visit Carrie.

By the end of the week, when she was able to get away, she had allowed herself to worry about Carrie and the decision to the point that she was beginning to feel ill. If Lemuel had known about it, he would have laughed and told her she took everything too seriously. But he didn't know about any of it. He was, as his mother had warned her, too involved with his own life and career. Perhaps it was true that she was taking it too seriously. Yet she knew that it was impossible not to take it seriously, not only because it had a direct bearing on her work, but beyond that, she also feared that Carrie was unfairly becoming a sacrifice to an ideology.

A week later, she arrived in Lynchburg and made her way from the train station to Madison Heights and the Colony. Carrie was neither in her kitchen workplace nor in the dorm. Louisa was told she was on her break time. She found her sitting alone on a bench on one of the lawns, bundled against the cold.

"Carrie?" she called as she approached her from her back.

Carrie didn't respond, although Louisa was certain she must have heard her. She called out again, but there was still no response. When she reached the bench, Louisa sat down next to Carrie, who glanced at her but said nothing.

"Are you all right?" Louisa asked.

Carrie turned her face away from her.

"Of course you're not all right. That was a silly question. I wanted to see you, Carrie. I wanted to tell you how—"

"I don't want to talk to you," Carrie said.

"I know how you must be feeling, but—"

"No you don't. How could you know how I feel? It's not happening to you."

Louisa felt too chastened to speak at first. "I'm sorry," she finally managed to say.

Carrie snorted derisively. "No you're not. You think it's best for me. You think I'm feebleminded. Well, maybe I am. I reckon I'm a long way from being as smart as you, but..." Her voice trailed off, and she stood and walked a few steps away.

"The case will be appealed. These things always are. A higher court could decide in your favor."

Carrie glanced at her. "What would be in my favor? Keeping me here? Or fixing me so I can't have more babies?"

Louisa knew she was right. Carrie would lose either way. "Well, if they go through with it, it *will* be your ticket out of here, just as you said. You can go back to the Dobbses. I understand they want you back. You'll be able to be with your daughter, and—"

"No," Carrie said, whirling around suddenly. "They changed their minds. They don't want me. At first they said they'd take me back, but then they sent a letter saying they decided they're gettin' too old to see after me, and the superintendent said it's best I don't try to be around Anna...around the baby."

Louisa felt stricken. She wanted to say something to Carrie, but she couldn't speak, and she felt herself shaking. She tried to stand to go to her, but a swarm of whirling lights pushed her back. Suddenly she couldn't see anything because the world was black.

When she opened her eyes again, she realized she was lying on the ground and Carrie was hovering over her calling her name, telling her to wake up. She felt something in her mouth, restricting her. She pulled it out and flung it across the winter-brown lawn.

"What was that nasty thing in my mouth?" she asked, spitting and crying.

"It was just a stick, Miss," Carrie said.

"A stick!"

"I had to put it in your mouth to keep you from swallowing your tongue."

Louisa stared at her in disbelief. "What? What are you saying?"

"I think you had a fit, Miss." Carrie was trying to help her up.

"A fit?"

"I think they call it a seizure here at the Colony," Carrie said. "It was a fit. An epileptic fit."

Louisa was on her feet, but she felt tired and almost couldn't make it to the park bench. She tried to speak, but she could only cry weakly.

"Don't worry; I won't tell nobody, Miss Van Patten. You don't want to end up here. Just go on home and don't say anything to nobody. I won't either."

"Carrie—"

"Can you make it back to the train station?"

"I...I don't know. If I could have a taxi..."

"I'll get you one. Just stay where you are," Carrie said.

Before Louisa could reply, Carrie was running across the lawn, away from her. She was back a few minutes later. "I had to go to the office to use the phone. I told 'em you wasn't feeling well and decided to leave early. That woman in front of the office wanted you to see the doctor, but you got lucky. He's not here."

"I...I don't understand how...what...How can I thank you, Carrie? How can I ever repay—"

"Hush now, Miss. It'll be all right. Don't fret now. Don't try to talk. Just save your energy."

With Carrie's help, Louisa got to the taxi that took her to the train station. She didn't go back to Bryn Mawr though. She went straight to New York and called her mother, who sent a driver to bring her home. Her mother put her to bed immediately and promised to call the doctor.

Dr. Haroldson, the family physician, still had not arrived when her father came home.

"Louisa!" he said, looking harried as he burst into her room.

"Hello, Father."

"Your mother called me, and I came as soon as I could." He looked behind him and around the room and then closed the door. "Tell me what happened. Your mother said you had a..." His voice trailed off, and he stood beside Louisa's bed, staring at her with a tormented look on his face as he twirled the brim of the hat he held in his hands.

"It seems I had a seizure," Louisa said. "Mother has called Dr. Haroldson. He should have been here by now. I want an examination to make certain of what happened."

She saw her parents exchange a look, but they said nothing.

"Why don't you call the doctor again, Father? I don't understand why he hasn't come."

Her father made no move to go downstairs to the telephone. He simply looked at her, still twisting his hat.

"Father, please go—"

"There's no need to call the doctor, Louisa."

"What?"

"You had a seizure, an epileptic seizure. It's not the first time, but we thought—"

"Not the first time? What do you mean?"

There was a long pause. "You had the first one when you were two. The doctor examined you then and said it was...said it was epilepsy. Then he confirmed it when you were four, and it happened again."

Louisa was stunned. "No! No, that can't be. I don't remember—"

"You don't remember, I know, but he confirmed both times that it is epilepsy," her father said. "He warned it could happen again, but we thought since it's been so long, . . .well, Dr. Haroldson thought the same thing. That maybe you'd outgrown it."

"Why didn't you tell me?" Louisa's voice was choked with anger.

"There was no need," her father said. "We thought you'd outgrown—"

"No need? Of course there was a need. It's my right to know about my health! Damn you!" She pounded the bed with her fist. "It could have been dangerous for me if I had a fit when I was alone."

Her mother tried to take her in her arms, but Louisa brushed her away.

"Not a fit, Louisa. A seizure." Her father's mouth hardened as he spoke.

"The most important thing is that I planned to have children! Were you simply going to let me pass my condition on to them?"

"There's no reason to think it is hereditary." Her father had stopped twirling his hat and stood straight and stoic. "No one on either side of my family or your mother's has been known to have the affliction."

"You're not a doctor, Father. Your observation proves nothing." Louisa swung her legs over the side of the bed as she spoke. "Now, if you'll excuse me, I have things to do."

Her mother caught her arm. "Louisa, you must rest. Please, you can't—"

"I have to go, Mother." She snatched her clothes from the chair where she'd left them when her mother put her to bed.

"There's nowhere you have to go," her father said. It sounded like an order.

"I have to see Lemuel," she answered, turning suddenly to face him. "He has a right to know."

Her father's face turned dark red with anger. "Think about what you're doing, Louisa. Think of all we have to lose!"

"What we have to lose? How can you—"

"It's been so long since the last seizure," her father said, making an attempt to calm down. "There's no reason for it to become public."

"I told you, Father, Lemuel has a right to—"

"We have a right, too, Louisa!" he said, interrupting her. "A right to privacy. You don't want a scandal. If it has to be dealt with later, we'll do that, but for now, think of the family, the Van Patten name."

"Stop it! I can't believe you're saying this." She turned away and started for the door again.

"Louisa, wait!"

Louisa dressed quickly in the bathroom and then hurried down the stairs to find her mother waiting for her. She paused a moment and kissed her mother on the cheek, whispered goodbye, and reached for the door.

"Louisa," her mother called to her, "I don't want to lose you."

"You haven't lost me, Mother," she said, turning back to her, "but I'll be gone a while. I have to start over, you see. I have to find a new road."

She spent the night in a hotel near the train station, and by the time the train arrived in Richmond, it was late the next evening. She went first to Lemuel's office, thinking he might be working late. She was right, and he was surprised to see her.

"Louisa! What...Are you all right?" He sprang from his chair and walked around the desk to grasp her shoulders.

"Aren't you glad to see me?"

"Of course." He pulled her close and kissed her. "You're not all right," he said, pulling back from what Louisa knew was not her usual response to his kiss. "Is something wrong?"

"I'm afraid so," she said. "You'd better sit down."

When she finished the story, she felt drained, and Lemuel's face was ashen. The drained feeling worried her for a moment, but she felt no further signs of a seizure. Lemuel seemed unable to speak.

"Louisa, I...I...this is... He stood and walked to his desk, keeping his back to her.

"It's all right, Lemuel. I know we can't go through with it." Her voice was soft but steady.

He turned to face her, his expression anguished. He opened his mouth to speak, but no words came out.

"It's believed to be hereditary, so of course I understand."

She waited, wondering if he would say it didn't matter, knowing she was foolish even to consider it and wondering if it even mattered to her now. She watched as he turned his back to her again.

She walked to the door and left his office.

To: Ben Newman
c/o New York Times
From: Louisa Van Patten, Charlottesville, Virginia
January 1925

Dear Ben,

You are no doubt surprised to see that I am writing to you from Charlottesville rather than Bryn Mawr. I am here with the intent of spending as much time with Carrie Buck as possible so I can get to know her better. I hope to be able to explain this to you in person when I come to New York next week. As to when I will return to my studies, I am not at all certain.

I expect to be in New York in two weeks, and I would like to see you. There is much I want to share with you. I won't be staying with my parents as I usually do. Instead, I will be staying at the Algonquin. Feel free to leave a message at the desk as to when and where we can meet.

I look forward to seeing you.

Affectionately,
Louisa

"Three generations of imbeciles are enough."

—Supreme Court Justice Oliver Wendell Holmes
in majority opinion of Supreme Court in Buck v. Bell, May 2, 1927

October 19, 1927
Virginia State Colony for the Epileptics and Feebleminded.

Patient, Carrie Buck was sterilized this morning under authority of Act of Assembly. . .providing for the sterilization of mental defectives and as ordered by the Board of Directors of this institution. She went to the operating room at 9:30 and returned at 10:30, recovered promptly from anesthesia with no untoward after effects anticipated. One inch was removed from each fallopian tube, the tubes litigated, and the end cauterized by carbolic acid followed by alcohol, and the ends of the broad ligaments brought together with continuous suture. Abdominal wound was united with layer sutures, and the approximation of closure was good.

To: Paula Paul, Albuquerque, New Mexico
From: Anna Newman Matvey, Phoenix, Arizona
May 29, 1987

Dear Ms. Paul,

I appreciate your interest in the part my mother played in the case of Carrie Buck, who was sterilized in Virginia in 1927, the year before I was born. My mother, Louisa Van Patten Newman, became quite close to Miss Buck, who later became Mrs. William Eagle and then, after Mr. Eagle's death, Mrs. Charles Detamore.

When Carrie was paroled from what was then known as the Colony in Madison Heights, she worked as a housemaid in various small towns in Virginia until her marriage. My mother visited her frequently at first, until Mother moved to Arizona. (She always referred to it as "fleeing to the desert.") That was in January 1928. Mother loved telling the story of how my father, Ben Newman, tracked her down using what she always called "sorcery." I was born in October of that year.

Mother continued to write to Carrie over the years and visited her at least twice that I know of. The first time was shortly after she learned that her daughter, Vivian, had died. Mother took Carrie to the gravesite. That was in 1933. Vivian had died of complications from measles in 1932, but Carrie was not notified for several months. Mother went to the trouble of looking up Vivian's school records and learned that she was very bright. Carrie, though uneducated, was also bright. I can attest to that because I have read all of the letters she wrote to my mother over the years. I know that Carrie frequently wrote to her own mother at the Colony and sent her money. She also made an effort to stay in touch with her brother and sister. Her sister, Doris, was also sent to the Colony and was sterilized, although she apparently was no more feebleminded than Carrie was.

The book you mentioned must have been the manuscript called *The Study of the Mind of a Deviant Woman*. I know little about it, except that Mother never finished it. I heard the title mentioned a few times when she was talking with Dad, but she didn't like to talk about it with me. After her death in 1980, I found a few notes relating to the manuscript and was able to determine that the book dealt with sterilization of the so-called feebleminded. When I was in college, I asked to read it, but she claimed to have misplaced the unfinished manuscript. I believe she burned it.

While she never finished writing her book, she did complete her degree in psychology and sociology and had a career as a social worker on Indian reservations here in Arizona.

Mother died peacefully in her sleep after suffering a stroke. You asked about her general health before her death, and I assume you were referring to her epilepsy. She told me she had experienced two seizures in early childhood and two more before she and my father were married but none after that. She warned me that epilepsy could be hereditary, but I have no signs of the disease and neither do my three children.

My father never finished his big exposé about the Buck trial he was writing for the paper he worked for in New York. He often teased Mother that the reason he didn't was because he had to drop everything to scour the country looking for her. My father died in Germany in 1941 just before the US became involved in the war. He went there to try to rescue his parents from the Nazi regime and keep them from being sent to a concentration camp with other Jews. He and his parents were killed trying to escape a train bound for a death camp.

Ironically, the Virginia sterilization law that brought my parents together was used as a model for the Hereditary Health Law, espoused by Adolf Hitler, that evolved into the atrocities of the Holocaust. Unfortunately, my mother always felt she had to take part of the blame. She carried that burden to her grave.

When I learned of Carrie's death six years ago, I went back for her funeral, a simple graveside service. She is buried in the same cemetery as her daughter, but there is a wide canyon that separates them.

In answer to your final question, yes, my name is Annabelle, although I've been called Anna since my college days. No, I do not know the significance of that name. I would appreciate any information you can give me.

Sincerely,
Anna Newman Matvey

AUTHOR'S NOTE

The Mind of a Deviant Women is a work of fiction based on the story of Carrie Buck, who was sterilized in 1926 in Virginia for being feebleminded and morally deficient. The sterilization took place after a trial to determine whether or not the act was constitutional. Its constitutionality was affirmed by the Supreme Court of the United States, and the law has never been repealed.

Many of the characters in this book were actual, living people. Some were created by my imagination. All of them are real to me.

QUESTIONS AND TOPICS FOR DISCUSSION

1. How likely would Carrie Buck be considered below average in intelligence today?

2. Are there parallels with today's discussions regarding abortion to those regarding sterilization in the early twentieth century?

3. Why was Annabelle, both the doll and the child, so significant to Carrie?

4. Why do you think Emma never tried to get Carrie back when she fought so hard at first to keep Doris and Roy from being taken from her?

5. Carrie never made a strong effort to get Annabelle/Vivian back. Why do you think she didn't?

6. How would you answer Ben's question, "Who gets to decide?"

7. Sterilization is still used for some mentally challenged individuals today. How valid is the argument for this practice?

8. If Louisa had never become aware of her own history of epilepsy, do you think she would have changed her mind about forced sterilization?

9. What do you think were the most dominate factors in Ben's opinion about eugenics?

10. What do you consider the most important theme of the novel?

BIBLIOGRAPHY

Baughman, Judith S., ed. *American Decades 1920–1929.* Detroit, MI: Gale Research, 1996.

Carpenter, Theresa, ed. *New York Diaries.* New York: Modern Library, Random House, Inc., 2012.

Chesterton, G. K. *Eugenics and Other Evils.* London, New York, Toronto, Melbourne: Cassell and Company, Limited, 1922.

Circuit Court of Amherst County, Buck v. Bell, Statement of Evidence November 18, 1924 (transcript of trial).

Gordon, Lois, and Alan Gordon. *The Columbia Chronicles of American Life 1910–1992.* New York: Columbia University Press, 1995.

Hall, Lee. *Common Threads: A Parade of American Clothing.* Boston, Toronto, London: Little, Brown and Company, 1992.

Lombardo, Paul A. *Three Generations, No Imbeciles*: *Eugenics, the Supreme Court, and Buck v. Bell.* Baltimore: Johns Hopkins University Press, 2008.

Penny, Darby, and Peter Stastny. *The Lives They Left Behind: Suitcases from a State Hospital Attic.* New York: Bellevue Literary Press, 2008.

Sanger, Margaret. *The Pivot of Civilization.* New York: Bretano's, 1922.

Smith, J. David, and K. Ray Nelson. *The Sterilization of Carrie Buck: Was She Feebleminded or Society's Pawn?* Far Hills, NJ: New Horizon Press, 1989.

Supreme Court of the United States, File No. 31, 681. Filed February 6, 1926, October term, 1926, No. 292, Buck v. Bell.

Tompkins, Vincent, ed. *American Decades 1910–1919.* Detroit, MI: Gale Research, 1996.